Teens Love THINGS CHANGE

"I just wanted to tell you just how much I loved your book *Things Change*. It made me laugh, it made me cry, and most importantly it made me think."
—Sarah, *age fifteen, Connecticut*

"I loved Johanna in all of her nerdy glory before she met Paul. You actually captured an insecure teenage girl very well, and since I highly doubt you've ever been an insecure teenage girl, I was really surprised because Johanna could be someone at my school."
—Amber, *age sixteen, Pennsylvania*

"I'm a person who hates to read. I've only read about five books in the past eight years. When I saw this book, I read the cover and decided that this would be a book I would buy. I started reading, and I couldn't put it down . . . I stayed up until three in the morning just to finish it!"
—Jen, *age fourteen, New York*

"I just finished reading *Things Change* and I believe this may be one of the truest fiction novels I have ever read. My ex-boyfriend was abusive and, like Paul, always promised to stop. I enjoyed this book, and it will sit on my shelf forever."
—Hannah, *age sixteen, Nebraska*

"I just got out of a bad relationship where some of the things my boyfriend said to me were exactly like Paul. About five days ago, my best friends gave me the book *Things Change*. I hate reading. It just doesn't interest me. But I finished it in three days. I want to read it again so badly, but the way I have been talking about it, all my friends want to read it. So I'm passing it on."
—Kaylee, *age thirteen, New Jersey*

More praise for

THINGS CHANGE

A 2005 Quick Pick for Reluctant Young Adult Readers

"A debut novel that is both forceful and cautionary."
—*Booklist*

"From the ironic title to the uncompromising ending,
tension dragged me by the hair through *Things Change* by Patrick Jones.
The details are revealed relentlessly and steadily, with each twist tightening
the noose of obsession, neediness, abuse, and control. . . . There is humor
here, but it's mixed with a darker seam, which I found intriguing.
I don't think I'll ever listen to Springsteen the same way again."

—ANNETTE CURTIS KLAUSE, author of *Blood and Chocolate*

"In his passionate first novel, noted librarian Patrick Jones
examines the one constant in young adult lives: change! And he does it
beautifully—with compelling insight; dramatic empathy; and
unsentimental, tough-minded but sympathetic understanding.
Things Change is a transformative reading experience,
and I wouldn't change a word of it."

—MICHAEL CART, former president of YALSA and author of
My Father's Scar and *Necessary Noise*

"The stakes for a young human being to come of age are always high,
but in Patrick Jones's *Things Change* the stakes are mortal. It's an important
novel for young readers—young women and men—and for their parents."

—TERRY DAVIS, author of *If Rock and Roll Were a Machine*

THINGS CHANGE

PATRICK JONES

WALKER & COMPANY
NEW YORK

To Dr. Erica Klein —P. J.

First published in the United States of America in 2004 by
Walker Publishing Company, Inc.
First paperback edition published in 2006

For information about permission to reproduce selections from
this book, write to Permissions, Walker & Company,
104 Fifth Avenue, New York, New York 10011

The Library of Congress has cataloged the hardcover edition as follows:
Jones, Patrick
Things change / Patrick Jones
p. cm
Summary: Sixteen-year-old Johanna, one of the best students in her class,
develops a passionate attachment for troubled seventeen-year-old Paul and
finds her plans for the future changing in unexpected ways.
ISBN-10: 0-8027-8901-3 • ISBN-13: 978-0-8027-8901-3 (hardcover)
[1. Interpersonal relations—Fiction.   2. Dating violence—Fiction.
3. Emotional problems—Fiction.   4. Self-perception—Fiction.
5. Mothers and daughters—Fiction.]   I. Title.
PZ7.J7242Th.   2004   [Fic]—dc22   2003057681
ISBN-10: 0-8027-7746-5 • ISBN-13: 978-0-8027-7746-1 (paperback)

Book design by Maura Fadden Rosenthal/Mspaceny

Visit Walker & Company's Web site at www.walkeryoungreaders.com

Printed in the United States of America

4 6 8 10 9 7 5 3

All papers used by Walker & Company are natural, recyclable products
made from wood grown in well-managed forests. The manufacturing processes
conform to the environmental regulations of the country of origin.

Thanks to teens in Eden Prairie, Minnesota, and Mesa, Arizona, who read the manuscript; thanks to Jessica M., Renee V., Erin P., Sarah C., Amy A., Maureen H., and Diane T. for their help, and kudos to Brent, Patricia, and Ken "the Slack" Rasak for their invaluable contributions.

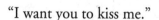

"I want you to kiss me."

Paul almost drove his black Firebird off the road when he heard those words come from my mouth. He pushed the blond hair out of his eyes as he turned to look at the lips that had just told him they wanted to be kissed. Turning the volume up on the CD player to push the loud, crashing sounds through the open windows and out into the cool September Michigan air, he stared straight ahead at the interstate before him, ignoring the question chasing behind him.

I shifted in my seat, digging my short, well-chewed finger-nails into the upholstery. I pulled a deep breath into my lungs and prepared to repeat the statement. This was more difficult than the first time. It was like being knocked down by a punch, only to come back with, "Thank you, sir. May I have another?" I was being Daddy's perfect, tough little marine girl.

"I want you to kiss me."

Softer now. The words vanished into the silence as Paul ejected the CD from the player. The silence was broken by Paul slapping the senior-class ring jammed on his finger against the steering wheel as he pulled the car off the interstate onto the shoulder. I just stared at the floor of the car, wishing I could take it all back.

"I'm sorry," Paul said gently, "but I don't want to kiss you." He stared straight ahead at the taillights of the passing cars as they disappeared over the horizon. It looked like they were falling off the end of the earth.

I wrapped my arms around myself as a chill shot through my body. I pulled my blazer tighter around me, trying to hold in any tears or hint of emotion.

"I just—" Paul started, but when his eyes met mine, the words choked back in his throat. He reached over to jam the CD back into the player. I was desperate now. Before he could move away, I, this girl he barely knew, reached out and gave his hand a light squeeze. I wanted to touch him; I wanted him to want to touch me. I forced the final attempt from the back of my throat and the front of my heart.

"Well, do you think you will *ever* want to kiss me?" I asked, choosing a tone that suggested amusement rather than disappointment or desire, trying to hide my desperation. I marked the end of the question by pushing the CD back into the player, turning the volume up to the max. I sat straight up in the seat, waiting, and bracing myself, for him to deliver the final blow.

Paul slammed the car back into drive, squealed the tires, and sped back out on the interstate. When the car kicked up to eighty miles per hour, he let out a small laugh. He never took his eyes off the gray asphalt stretching out before him as he shrugged his shoulders and said, with a hint of a smile, "Well, Johanna, things change."

TWO

"Aren't you a little late, Johanna? You're supposed to call when you're going to be late."

I had barely managed to get inside the door before my mother began her interrogation. It seemed when she spoke to me anymore, it was like Jeopardy: Her words always came in the form of a question.

"Why were you late?"

I focused my eyes on the carpet, hiding the fact I had dampened the sidewalk between the driveway and the front door with a few ounces of tears. "I had a student council meeting to cover for the school paper. I thought I told you."

"So who gave you a ride home?" my mother asked, peering out the window while taking a deep drag on her cigarette.

"Just someone from school," I said, the irony thick in my throat. Paul wasn't *someone;* he was the *only* person I had thought about all summer. I asked him for a ride home after the meeting, and as I had hoped, he said yes. If only he would have said yes to my second question.

"What do you have to say for yourself?" she asked, a Sphinx-like question she would ask most any time I did something to displease her or my father.

I didn't really know what answer she wanted from me. What

I mostly knew was that I hated her tone, hated her freakish need to control me, hated the way she made me feel like I was stupid. But mostly I hated my fear that I would disappoint her and my father.

"I don't like this at all," she said, the head shake followed by a frown announcing my failure.

My brain was working overtime trying to answer, not her question, but my own: How can people who said they loved you all the time make you hate them as much as I hated my mother right now. It hadn't always been this way, but since I'd hit high school, she had turned into this queen of control.

"Like I said, I'm sorry. I thought I told you," I replied, climbing up the first stair toward my room, trying to escape the inevitable showdown, which, of course, I never won.

"Don't you walk away. I'm talking to you, Johanna Marie!" Once my middle name was announced, it was like my mother was throwing down the gauntlet. I stumbled backward off the stair.

She stared me down. "If you're late, you're supposed to call, isn't that right?"

I stood mute. It was so humiliating to be treated like a stupid child when I am one of the smartest girls in the junior class. I know that sounds terrible, but it's true. Still, there are plenty of things I am not. Just by looking at the other girls in school, I know that I'm not as beautiful as some of them or as good with boys. I'm not even that good when it comes to making friends. That was a social study I had been failing for three years—except for my best friend, Pam. So I just stood and listened to my mother's attack. I couldn't run. I couldn't hide. All I could do is tough it out and take it, but she wouldn't see me cry. I learned a long time ago that fighting back just made it worse.

"Yes, Mother," I finally squeaked out in no more than a whisper. "I'll try to do better."

"Trying isn't good enough, understand?" she asked as she dismissed me with her eyes and a cloud of white smoke.

Lugging my overstuffed book bag behind me, I escaped up the stairs. I opened the door to my bedroom, tossed the weight of junior-year homework on the floor next to the bed, and dove facedown into my pillow. Within seconds tears were choking me. I was having trouble breathing, pulling the pillow tight against the side of my head to silence the sobbing and suffocate the hurt.

I rubbed my eyes, and then licked my fingertips to taste the tears. My grandmother told me when I was a little girl that tears, just like the ice cream I love eating, have different flavors. There is a flavor for anger, one for sadness, another for hurt, and a sweet flavor for love. That was a flavor I had yet to taste in my short sixteen years. I wouldn't go hungry this night for want of any flavor, but running together, they all tasted bitter. My stomach hurt from crying; my nose was running; I was a mess.

I reached down beside the bed and pulled up my stuffed book bag to find a tissue. All those books, all that knowledge, and all of it useless to me now. What I really needed wasn't in these books: I needed the formula to invent a time machine. Then I could go back in time and erase the past few hours from life—and from Paul's memory. I would still have a crush on him, but he wouldn't know it or care. Life would go back to normal: He wouldn't know I existed, and I would continue to exist stuck between the rock and the hard place, living between my feelings of wanting and waiting. Waiting and wanting.

THREE

Dear Dead Dad:

It's Paul, again.

I am sitting here with you all around me.

I'm drunk, big surprise. I am dead drunk. You are just dead.

I'm sitting here, like most nights so far during this, my glorious senior year, in the black cold of the white walls in room 127 of the Atlas Mini-Storage. I've got a six-pack, or what is left of it. I'm sitting here with my life, or what is left of it. Seventeen years old and you are five and a half years gone from my life and three years gone from this world.

Sometimes I think I know everything. I just want to shout, kick, scream, and slam because I know it all, I want it all, I need it all.

Sometimes, like right damn now, I just want to shout, kick, scream, and slam because I don't know anything. Stone-cold stupid, but not stone-cold sober.

Bouncing back and forth is beating me down: like work, like school, like Mom, like this thing with

this girl Johanna. So she wants to kiss me. I've
been thinking about all the things I should have
said. All the things I could have said. But I should
have just asked her one thing: Why? If she's so
smart, why would she want to kiss me? I am nothing.

I wonder what she is doing right now. I don't
know, but I'm pretty sure she's not sitting in the
near darkness of a six-by-six mini-storage room,
downing a six of Stroh's. The only light is this
computer screen and a single bulb hanging overhead
in this, my temporary shelter.

Thanks to you, the shelter Mom and me live in is
a trailer in the Garden Oaks Trailer Park, except
there are no oaks, there are no gardens, there are
just trailers. Temporary housing that no one gets
out of. Is that what death does, Dad? Does it get
your soul out of the temporary housing of your body?
Is your body just another trailer?

I am sitting here with you all around me.

I always want to ask Mom why she kept your stuff.
She has her reasons, but she never talks about them.
She never talks about you at all. She saved most
everything: your clothes, your tools, your music.
That music saved me.

I needed a part of you. I didn't know what part.
Then I found it. I learned everything I needed to
learn listening to your Springsteen CDs. I found you
there. It is a regular father-and-son picnic in my
head, with guitar, bass, and drum. LOUD. I thought
if I listened to the same music that I would get

close to you. That I would know you. That you would
know me.

This is my secret life, here at the Atlas Mini-
Storage. No one knows about it. I just lie to Mom.
Tell her that I work until eleven, and then when I
get off at nine, I get some beer if I can, and I
come here. I want to tell Brad about it. I thought
about bringing Carla here, and I dream of bringing
Vickie here. I want to share it. But for now, it is
our secret.

No one else is ever here. I come in, punch in the
secret code, get in the gate, punch in another
secret code, open the front door, and then unlock
the door to room 127. If Mom ever noticed the key
missing, she never told me; but then we don't talk
much anyway.

She tries, I guess. When you left, she didn't
know what to do. She cried a lot, especially when
we lost the house. Then she found Jesus. She doesn't
cry anymore, but she seems pretty clueless about
life. About me. She thinks Jesus loves me. She
thinks I'm at work. Well, I am.

I am working out my life in the darkness of the
Atlas Mini-Storage, in the light of a Dell computer
and one lonely lightbulb, and under the power and
the glory of the yeast and the hops of the Stroh's
Brewing Company, Detroit, Michigan.

The music is crashing into my ears, but mostly I
hear silence. The buzz of the beer should be making
me feel good, but mostly I feel lousy. I ask all

these questions, but I get no answers. I want my father, but instead I have boxes of clothes and trinkets from your life. Just trinkets. I am sitting here with you all around me, but I don't know you and you don't know me.

Well that, and Springsteen, and the beer, I guess, are the things we have in common because I don't know me, either. Only Brad knows me. After I dropped off that Johanna girl at her house, I called Brad and met up with him at our usual.

He's real busy with Kara and school and the paper, but he's always there for me. After we graduate, we're going to leave this town for losers and head to California. We flew out there a couple of summers ago to visit his older brother, and that cemented it. He's taking hard classes like Latin and honors physics so he can get into Stanford by showing what a great scholar he is. I'm taking easy stuff so I can get into Stanford by just having decent grades, since my SATs suck.

We've been best friends since junior high, since you left. Other kids at school are always changing the people they hang with, but Brad and I don't change. He's a rock. He spends a lot of time with Kara. To hear him tell it, most of it is spent horizontal. Me, I spend time at work and here in room 127 of the Atlas Mini-Storage. Brad doesn't know about this place and these letters to you. It's my secret, and not my only one, either. Like what happened with Carla. He suspects, but even if he

knew, he would never tell. He told me once that he
was with me, right or wrong.

 We get together at Supreme Donuts down the street
from the old engine plant you worked at every now and
then. Over the strange brew that is Supreme Donuts
coffee, I told Brad about Johanna. I figured since he
took journalism class with her that he might know
what was going on. He had been hinting to me that she
was interested, but my interest is Vickie.

"Hey, you know that brainy girl, Johanna?" I asked as I finished
off a glazed doughnut.

"Let me see; I edit the school paper, and she's the assistant editor. What do you think?"

"So, I'm driving her home and—"

"Why are you driving her home?" Brad asked with a huge
smile on his face.

"She was at that stupid student council thing you dared me
to do. Thanks a lot, bro."

"My pleasure." Brad smiled.

"So she asked for a ride, and I thought what the hell. So, I'm
Firebirding her home, and she says out of nowhere, 'I want you
to kiss me.'"

"Get out of town!" Brad almost spilled his coffee.

"I couldn't believe it."

"Paul, I've been telling you that she likes you. She's always asking me stuff about you. She's always trying to get your attention."

"Well, it looks like she did," I said as I sipped my coffee.

"But she got it all wrong. She should put one hand on your

shoulder and the other hand in your pants, that would've got you to stand at attention," Brad said.

"Funny man, real funny." Nobody cracked me up like Brad.

"I wasn't joking. So, how was it?"

"I said no." I looked down at my Chucks when I said it.

"What's with that?"

"I don't know, bro. She caught me off guard, and I was a little bit—"

"Afraid? Get over it, Paul. Now, if it were me—"

"If it were you, she would have to take a number. And Kara would kill her," I replied.

Brad laughed. "Both are points well-taken."

"I don't think Johanna is what I want," I mumbled. "She's smart and all, but—"

"You still want Vickie. Talk about taking a number. You'd better give that up."

"Now, why wouldn't Vickie say something like that to me?" I asked with a smile.

"Listen, bro, I think you should tell Johanna that you blew it. You say yes; she'll say yes; and before you know it, you'll be banging each other's brains out," Brad said.

"I'm not thinking about her like that," I said.

"Like hell you aren't. Listen. You're seventeen; I'm seventeen. This is how we think."

"I still want Vickie, but she just wants to be good friends."

"Then do something to change that. Force the issue; you have nothing to lose," Brad said firmly. In ways of women, I followed his advice one hundred percent.

"So how do I get Vickie to put her hand in my pants?" I said as I threw some change on the table.

"You're not serious," Brad said, taking his final sip of coffee.

"Brad, tell me this: In the almost six years we've known each other, have you ever known me not to be serious?"

"Only most of the time."

"Well, then maybe it's time for a change," I told him as we walked out the door.

But now Dad, none of that seems funny anymore; sometimes nothing does. There is so much stuff I am trying to work out, and I am doing it all alone.

You left me. You decided to leave. You know what you did. I know what you did to me and to Mom. And I know that I miss you.

Dad, I would offer you a beer, but like you, they are all gone.

FOUR

"So, who is this who gave you a ride home yesterday?" Even first thing in the morning my mother was in questioning mode, her caffeine and nicotine fixes kick-starting her day. She was attired in one of her many tailored suits, perfectly dressed and made up for her workday.

"His name is Paul. He's a senior at my school," I said, stifling a yawn. I'd slept very little. I had kept looking over at the alarm clock, the red letters announcing each minute of sleeplessness passing by. I spent most of the night staring up at the ceiling, memorizing every square inch like a math formula, unable to relax or sleep.

"So, JoJo, does he play any sports?" my father asked, sitting down next to me and passing me a glass of orange juice.

I tried not to laugh, because Paul seemed so anti-jock. Not laughing was easy enough, since humor wasn't a big feature of our little household. Every morning was similar to this one: a nice family breakfast with my father's face buried in the *Wall Street Journal,* my mother's face buried in my business, and me trying to face another day. "No, he's on the student council."

"A politician. Just what the world needs, another politician," my father grunted.

"So, do you like this boy?" my mother asked.

"Mom, he just gave me a ride home," I said, grabbing a piece of the newspaper so I could hide my eyes from my mother.

I wanted to be able to talk with her about Paul and about lots of things, but it just never happened anymore. While there were still things we did together, like play Scrabble or go shopping for clothes, something had changed since I started high school. I felt less like a daughter she was raising and more like a project she was managing. She was proud of me, bragged about me to all the relatives, and to her friends and coworkers, about how well I did at school; but sometimes it seemed to be more about her than me. She and my dad always told me they were proud of me; they told me they love me. But love in our family was like a bad novel: all tell and no show.

She ground out her cigarette in the ashtray. "Well, I don't see how you really have time for this Paul character. Don't you have the SATs coming up in a few weeks?"

"But Mom, I took the PSATs last year and got almost a perfect score," I said.

"Horseshoes and hand grenades," my father said from behind his paper. Close wasn't good enough. I guess since I was their only child, only perfection was expected.

"So this year, if you study hard, you can get a perfect score," my mother said. "Wouldn't that be great, honey?"

"My little girl will do just fine. She always does. Besides, I wouldn't expect any less." My father put his paper down, smiled, and gave my hand a tender squeeze. My dad saw himself as tough but fair, and he normally was. My mother, well, I don't know how she saw herself. Looking at her lately was like looking at a fun-house mirror: I wasn't getting the real reflection of her, just this distorted image. The more she treated me like I was still twelve, the more I tried to pretend I was twenty. It was simple physics: she pushed, and I pulled away.

I wanted to shout out how no one was perfect, but then I thought about Vickie, the girl at school who, unlike me, had captured Paul's attention. Maybe if I looked like Vickie, he would notice me. Vickie looks like the homecoming queen that she is, with her perfect blond hair and blue eyes, her perfect body, perfect everything. I hate her. It isn't fair. I'm smart, so why doesn't that matter? I see how Paul looks at Vickie; I see how he never looks at me. Getting a perfect score on the SATs wasn't going to change that. Or maybe if I looked like Brad's chic but spacey girlfriend, Kara, Paul would have answered yes to my question.

"He's not another one of these troublemakers, is he?" my father asked, putting down his paper long enough to pour himself another cup of coffee.

"I don't think so," I said, trying to hide my smile. Paul was often in trouble at school, mainly for being such a cutup in class or at assemblies. He seemed so assertive, even aggressive at times, so I thought he would like that quality in me. I guess I was wrong.

"JoJo, you are better than that," my dad said.

I didn't answer. I didn't like to talk about Ty, who had been my last/first/only boyfriend. After Ty dumped me in May, my dad said he didn't want to see me with those types. It was right after that parental pronouncement, however, that I developed my crush on Paul.

"There are more important things you should be doing with time," my mother added.

"I know," I agreed, which almost killed me, but they were probably right. I think they knew that Ty would hurt me. I think they knew, and they let it happen to teach me a lesson: that they were right. Sometimes I think what hurt the worst wasn't Ty dumping me, but my mother's I-told-you-so look for months after.

"Don't know what you ever saw in that loser, anyway." My father got his shot in, and then retreated back behind the newspaper again.

"He liked me," I said, trying to make the complex sound simple. The truth, they didn't want to hear: Ty said he wanted me. Maybe that was enough.

"Whatever happened to him?" my mother asked. It seemed a question of courtesy rather than true curiosity.

I shifted in my chair, taking the last bite out of my bagel. "He dropped out of school."

"Like I said, trouble," my father interjected.

"You'll have time for this after you graduate from college, won't you?" my mother asked, but allowed no time for an answer. "Your friends don't have boyfriends now, do they?"

"I guess not," I said, quickly grabbing another bagel to stuff in my mouth so I wouldn't be drawn into yet another topic of conversation I wanted to avoid: my friends, or lack thereof. I'm in a lot of clubs at school, but those people are not my friends. When the meetings are over, they go their way, usually together, and I go mine. The boys in my honor classes aren't interested in me. I guess they feel threatened or something. The girls in those classes I thought would be my friends, but they've sent a clear message that their clique is at quota. A couple of the girls, and I find this hard to believe, are even more socially awkward and shy than me. But I want something different; I guess that was why I liked Ty, and now Paul.

"Your friend Pam doesn't have a boyfriend, does she?" my mother continued.

"No, she doesn't," I said, looking at my watch, thankful that Pam would be showing up any minute to rescue me from this morning ritual. I know my parents mean well, and I guess, unlike lots of kids at school who never talk with their parents, I am fortunate that we spend this time together. But sometimes, it is too much. "I've got to go."

I got up from the table, taking a last sip of juice, a hug from my father, and pro forma "Love you's" from the both of them. I gathered my heavy book bag and stood on the front porch waiting for Pam to drive me to school.

I met Pam soon after I transferred to Pontiac West High School during the middle of ninth grade. We had just moved from one nice house in the suburbs of Detroit to another, even nicer one. Good for my parents, climbing the golden stairs to success; bad for their daughter, starting a new school in the middle of the year. At lunch, people would come over and start to talk with me, but then somebody else, somebody they knew better, would come along, and I would be out of the conversation. After a while, I stopped eating lunch in the cafeteria. I got tired of sitting alone or sitting with people who included me in their conversations but not their lives. I would go to the newspaper room during lunch to work on stories or do homework. Sometimes, I would just go to the library, find a thick fantasy novel and a quiet corner, and read. That's how I met Pam. I was sitting in my usual corner, totally engrossed in the latest Tamora Pierce novel. Pam just appeared out of nowhere and said she'd read the same book, which started us talking. My parents might argue that we had not stopped talking since that day.

"What's up, Books?" asked Pam as I climbed in her car. It was a nickname I didn't really like, but I did almost always have a book in my hand.

I took a deep breath and launched into it. "I did something really stupid."

"I don't think that's possible," she replied.

"I got up the nerve to ask Paul to give me a ride home from school yesterday, and then I asked him if he wanted to kiss me."

"You did what?" she asked as we backed out of the driveway. She knew about my crush on Paul. Sometimes it would be all I talked about, but I didn't tell her of my little plan.

"He said no. I can't believe it. I am so stupid."

"So what are you going to do?" Pam asked. I knew Pam well enough to know it was a rhetorical question. In due time she would tell me what she would do and what I should do. Pam wasn't real big on life experience, but that never stopped her from giving advice.

I bit down hard on the thumbnail on my left hand. "I just wanted him to like me. That's all I wanted."

There was a pause. Pam knew I was lying. I didn't want him to like me. I wanted him to love me and think I was beautiful. I wanted to be like those other girls I saw at school with their boyfriends—laughing, kissing, being part of something other than the parent pride parade.

"Look at it this way," Pam said. "Anyone who wouldn't want to kiss you, you wouldn't want to have kiss you—get it?"

"I guess," I muttered.

"Look, I'm your best friend, right?" Pam started. "When Ty dumped you and you did your Humpty-Dumpty impersonation, who put you back together again?"

"It was you," I said. This was a ritual Pam needed. She liked
to remind me what a good friend she was. Like me, Pam seemed
in constant need of reassurance.

Pam continued. "So who's going to help you now?"

"You are."

"Books, be careful. Don't you think if he hurt you once, he'll
hurt you again?" Pam asked.

I sank down in my seat. "I just don't know what to do next."

"Show him that he can't hurt you and get away with it," Pam
said confidently.

My head was imploding, so my heart took over. It did what it
was supposed to do, acting as the body's most resilient and most
mysterious muscle. "But he can, Pam. He can."

FIVE

Mr. Taylor was standing in front of the class trying to get every-one's attention. It's a game we play most days at the beginning of my first-period journalism class.

"Excuse me, the bell rang five minutes ago," Mr. Taylor said in a voice not much louder than a whisper. "This is a tough bunch, Johanna. See what happens when you have so many cre-ative people in one room? I love it!"

I saw Brad sitting off to the side, drinking his normal big cup of coffee. Brad was gorgeous, just totally out of my league. You have to find your level, and Brad was well over mine. He had dark, curly brown hair; brown eyes; and he had a nicely trimmed mus-tache and beard, which looked great against the brown leather jacket he was wearing. Standing beside him were Lynne and Jackie, two of his girlfriend Kara's clique. Pam and I had dubbed them "the giggle girls" because they never seemed serious about anything but their clothes and makeup.

I kept looking over at Brad, trying to see if his face gave any indication that he knew what an idiot I'd been in the car with Paul. If he knew, he wasn't letting on. He just sat there oozing charisma and sipping his coffee.

"People, please. People." Mr. Taylor is a great person, but kids in the class know they can take advantage of him.

I stood and rapped a notebook against the desk. "I need everyone's attention, and I need you to look at the assignment sheets."

"The Chief said SHUT UP!" Brad screamed at the top of his lungs, even though his eyes remained squarely focused on the floor in front of him. Even though Brad was the editor of the paper, he called me "the Chief." He and Mr. Taylor let me have a lot of responsibility as the assistant editor, like making the story assignments.

"Hey, I want to write about the homecoming," Jackie said when she saw that she'd been assigned to write a story about the theater department's fall production.

"Homecoming is so lame," Tarsi, one of the Goth girls in class, hissed.

"It's so stupid," Erin, another princess of the night, added.

Jackie stood up and looked over at them. "How would you know? You'll never go."

Erin shouted across the room, "That's because I would rather be dead than—"

"Don't you think you're already dead?" Brad said, not missing a beat. Most everyone laughed, and the giggle girls were beside themselves.

"Don't worry," I said. "I'm taking this story, and I'll try to present both points of view."

Mr. Taylor looked up from his desk. He was smiling. He held up two fingers on each hand like a peace sign. "Remember, there are two sides to every story."

I don't think Mr. Taylor would be smiling, though, if he knew why I took the homecoming story. I wanted an excuse to learn more about Vickie, the shoo-in homecoming queen. The first day of the school year when I saw Brad, I asked him if Paul had a girl-friend. I don't remember how I phrased it, but I tried not to let on that I liked Paul. I made it seem like a casual question. He said, "Vickie, if you ask him."

I tried to bury myself in work, but I couldn't control my mind. I couldn't decide what I hated most about Vickie. It isn't real hate, just stupid envy. When she walked in the hall, she knew every boy, including Paul, was looking at her, while I walked through school like the invisible woman.

Vickie can't help that Paul wants her, but I always thought it was odd for him to like someone as normal and popular as Vickie. One of the things that attracted me to Paul was that he didn't seem to be like everyone else, from the way his blond hair hung halfway down his back to the pair of well-worn black high-top Converse All Stars he wore on his feet to the old beat-up Firebird that he parked in the same spot every morning. But mostly what I noticed was that whenever I see him, people are laughing. I think he holds the record for most times kicked out of the school library, which is where I first really noticed him one day last spring. He usually sits at a table with Brad, Kara, Jackie, Lynne, and some other seniors that I don't know, and within ten minutes everyone is laughing hysterically. I want to be a part of that, not stuck alone in the corner. I guess I will be today, since I'm sure they will all be laughing with my comic humiliation of the night before acting as the punch line.

"Johanna, you just can't please everyone." Mr. Taylor inter-rupted my mind wanderings. "It is all about balance. You did a good job with the assignments."

I could feel myself blushing. "Thanks," I blurted out. Although I wanted his approval, I felt so shy about getting it.

"Mr. Taylor, can I talk to you for a minute, in private?" I asked, avoiding eye contact.

"Is something wrong?" Mr. Taylor asked as we both stepped out into the hallway.

"I just wanted to ask you something." I was stalling. I couldn't come right out and ask him what I should do about Paul, but I needed some guidance. "I'm a little worried."

"Worried?" Mr. Taylor said in a tone that suggested he could take it all away. The way he looked at me filled me with confidence. It reminded me of my father's face when I do something that makes him proud. A little smile with the head cocked back slightly. The difference, of course, is it takes so little to please Mr. Taylor and so much to please my parents. I didn't know if his standards were too low or their standards were too high.

"What if there is a mistake in the paper?" I asked, hiding the real question.

Mr. Taylor smiled. "The best description of journalism was from Phil Graham who used to publish the *Washington Post*. He called journalism 'a first rough draft of history.'"

"A first rough draft of history." I repeated it. I liked that line.

"It's a draft. We do our best, we check our sources, we do everything we can to make sure it is perfect, but nothing is perfect. There will be mistakes." Mr. Taylor was in full teaching mode, the kind he did best: giving one-on-one lessons to those who cared rather than speaking to airheads like Jackie and Lynne trying to squeeze in an elective credit.

"But you can't correct those mistakes?" I asked. I think he knew that we were talking about something other than high school journalism.

"Johanna, there are very few mistakes that you can't overcome.

If you have a strong character, you can overcome just about any obstacle. Mistakes, you might say, are a test of character." Mr. Taylor's smile was as big as his heart.

"Let's say you want something really bad, and then you try to get it, but you make a mistake. What should you do?" I was asking it as clearly as I could without naming names.

Mr. Taylor shot a glance inside the classroom in response to the escalating noise. "From the way you asked the question, I think you know the answer. You might get knocked down, but stay focused and keep working toward your goals."

"I think you missed your calling, Mr. Taylor," I said with a smile on my face. "You should've been a football coach."

He looked into the classroom. "Now, if I could only discipline this team!"

He opened the door. The sound shot out of the room like a tidal wave, but my brain was noisily thinking about what Mr. Taylor had said. A test of character? So, was this whole thing with Paul, a test of character? I have never failed a test in my life and don't intend to start now.

SIX

Dear Dead Dad:
It's Paul, again. It's the middle of the day, and
I'm in the middle of some deep trouble.

I started this day looking to find Vickie and to
avoid Johanna. Knowing that Johanna wanted me somehow made me more convinced that I wanted Vickie. I
decided this morning that I would take matters into
my own hands regarding Vickie. (Well, as you and I
know, I'd taken something else into my own hands
thinking about Vickie many times.)

I waited for her outside her first-period class.
Other kids shuffled by, but I just looked through
them, staring at the clock in the hall. It seemed
like everything—everything in my life—hinged on
the next few minutes. If Johanna wanted to kiss me,
then maybe I wasn't such an ogre and loser after
all. I knew, too, that I was finally over Carla.
Hell, she never really mattered that much, anyway.
Carla was just a distraction; Vickie remained my
destiny. It was time to make my stand with her once
and for all.

"Vickie, hey, wait a minute." I pushed the words out but stared down at my Chucks. I wasn't ready for eye contact yet.

She barely broke stride as she looked up at the clock, saying, "Paul, I'm late for class."

"This is important, Vick. Gimme just a minute, please."

"Paul, I just don't have time right now."

I wanted to just shake her. Get in her face and shout: YOU NEVER HAVE TIME FOR ME, DAMN IT! But I held back that urge and instead gave my shoulders a slight shrug, trying to look sheepish and a little hurt, playing for sympathy. I finally looked up from my shoes and flashed my eyes right at her. "Vick, c'mon, just a minute."

Behind us I heard the door to her classroom slam shut.

"See, it doesn't matter now," I told her. "You're already late, so what is a few more minutes going to hurt? What are they gonna do, sic the tardy police on us? Maybe throw us a tardy party? If you are late again, does that mean you are a re-tardy? Besides, I'll write you a note. Your dad is a doctor, so I can fake his handwriting. Just gotta break a couple of fingers to make it that illegible."

"Paul, you're too much," she said with a laugh.

"Let's take a walk," I told her. Actually, if we got caught, I was sure I could talk my way out of it. I usually could.

"Where are we going?" she asked nervously. I was losing her.

"I would suggest we stop by the cafeteria to have something to eat; but as you know, food is not served in our cafeteria. That is, unless grease is recognized as one of the five basic food groups. If our cooks worked in a prison, a guy going to the chair would turn down his last meal."

We kept walking as I was letting go with the jokes. Finally, we reached a nice deserted hallway by the theater wing. It was about the only quiet place in the entire school. The school library was supposed to be quiet, but I usually had something to do with changing that.

"Really, Paul, I have to get to class," Vickie said with a sigh.

"All work and no play makes Vickie a tired little girl," I said, pulling one of the books out of the stack pressed up against that beautiful body. It was a guide to colleges. "Is Stanford in here?"

"I suppose. I just got that book," she said as I quickly flipped through the pages.

"There it is!" I said, opening the page to show her the description of Stanford.

"Is that where you're going?"

"Me and my bro Brad; the dynamic duo are California bound."

She glanced over and looked at the book. "Wow, that's expensive."

"I know, I know, I know," I said, shaking my head. "That's what I wanted to ask you. Could your dad loan me half a mil for the next four years?"

"What?" she asked quickly, and then she laughed. "Joking, right?"

"Listen, Vickie, this is a town full of losers, and I am pulling out of here to win." After I quoted the Boss, I got real agitated. I couldn't stop thinking how unfair everything was: She had so much, and I wanted just a little.

"Paul, you can be so melodramatic!"

"Look, I'm sorry." I touched her hands. "Let me make it up by having you come with me to Jackie's party tonight. Maybe we could go to Santi's for pizza before."

"What?" I think she actually looked stunned.

I kicked my ankles together, hard. "I gotta work, but I can be at your house—"

"Paul." Her tone said more than her words. "I can't go with you, you know that."

I stood there hearing my heart break for a moment. "Can't or won't?" I asked.

"Don't put it like that. I'm sorry, but why can't you be happy with us being friends? I really like you, but, you know, just not in that way," she said. "All I was saying—"

"Was the same damn thing you have been saying for three years!" Like a string that had been pulled too tight for too long, I felt something inside of me snap. It was as if all of my fears and frustrations were pulling in one direction, while what little self-control and discipline I possess were pulling in the other. It was no contest. "The same damn thing for three years."

I gave the wall a hard kick as Vickie backed away from me. She stood pressed against the yellow concrete. "Paul, don't go all postal on me. I like you, I like you a lot; but I just—"

"You just want to be friends." I kicked the wall again, missing Vickie's leg by inches.

"I don't want to go with you, okay?" When she said it, she sounded sorry; but it wasn't her pity that I wanted.

I leaned into her. I put my hands flat against the wall: my arms were like bars on a cage; she couldn't escape this time. "I don't want an apology. I just want you to like me, that's all."

"I DO like you, Paul. I can't explain why I don't like you *that* way."

"Sure you can; you're smart. Just look at all the books you carry," I said, then I grabbed the books pressing up against that body I would never get to touch and knocked them to the floor.

They sounded like a bomb as they smacked hard against the floor.

"Paul, please, don't be this way." She looked down at her books. "I'm sorry, okay?"

The echo of the books swallowed up her words, and the big silence returned. I grabbed her chin and pushed it up, making her look at me, then slapped my hands hard against the wall. "So am I, so am I."

"Paul, come on, please don't do that." She started to bend over to pick up her books. "Look, I know you're upset. Don't hurt yourself."

"But I am hurting. *You* are hurting me, Vickie." I starting kicking her books down the hall: world history, math, science, Latin, and the rest went sailing one by one across the cold floor, stopping with a thud against the concrete wall.

"Paul, this is too much." She started to walk away, turning her back to me.

"Too bad for you," I mumbled. I grabbed her hands and pulled her back toward me. "Look, Vickie, we're holding hands, just like you were my girlfriend. Don't you think that's funny?"

"Let go, let go!" I let go of her hands but pushed her hard against the wall.

"I guess it isn't that funny, but how about this?" I said as I raised my right hand above my head, forming a fist. Then with all the force in my body I brought it down hard against the wall, missing Vickie's face by inches. The red started running down my hand as Vickie ran down the hall.

I stood there for just a minute, the sound of her footsteps pushing the air out of my lungs into the emptiness of the hallway. I broke the silence and probably a couple of fingers as I began to swing at the wall until I couldn't stand the pain anymore. I kicked open the door at the end of the hall and ran toward the Firebird.

I jumped in the car, rolled down the windows, pushed the gas, squealed the tires, and threw in my *Born To Run* CD. I got it programmed to the title song (. . . *tramps like us, baby we were born to run*), and by the time I hit the interstate, I was ready to run away forever.

But then Dad, I looked in front of me and saw nothing but road. I looked in the rearview mirror and thought about the vacant stores and closed factories of my hometown, and then I drove a little faster. When I passed the city limits sign, it was like the wind got knocked out of me. I had everything to run from, but nothing and no one to run to, except maybe that Johanna girl. But first, I drove here for some quality father and son time. I drove here because I knew you would understand. I had nothing and no one to run to, except to you, Dad, a man who knew everything about running away.

SEVEN

"Paul?"

I had just stepped out of school to wait for Pam to drive me home from school when I saw Paul's black Firebird zip into the school lot. You could hear it coming: The only thing louder than the semidetached muffler was the music blaring through the open windows. He stopped right in front of me. When he got out of the car, he slammed the door loudly behind him.

"Shouldn't you be in class, little miss?" Paul yelled at me. He walked toward me and then pulled his glasses halfway down his nose and shook his finger back and forth in a dead-on impersonation of Mrs. Henderson, one of the school's vice-principals. "All students at Pontiac West High School have class! You must go to South High; now that is a school with no class."

I laughed, stopping when I noticed that Paul's right hand was wrapped up in a black do-rag that he sometimes wore on his head. I could see there was dried blood as far down as the wrist. He must have caught me looking because he quickly tucked his right hand into the pocket of his fatigues.

"This could earn you a total of five detentions, four demerits, three stay-afters, two written reprimands, and a partridge in a pear tree," he sang as used his left hand to readjust his glasses.

"But if you commit your next offense by homeroom, you'll win a brand-new car!"

This was strange. Was he pretending the other night didn't happen? Was I? Would I pass this test? What did he want me to say? "I don't need a car. I hate to drive."

"So why don't I give you a ride home again?"

"No, I have to wait for Pam and—"

He didn't say anything. He just bit his bottom lip, then shrugged his shoulders and walked back toward his car. He opened the passenger door, then waved me over. "Come on, climb in."

I took no time to answer, only the time it took to utter the words "first rough draft" to myself. I could apologize to Pam later. "Sure."

As soon as he sat down in his car, he pushed in a CD, then started the car. Before he turned the volume up, however, he leaned over toward me. I couldn't imagine what he was thinking. Looking him almost right in the eyes, I couldn't catch a clue to what he was feeling.

"This Bird is ready to fly!" Paul shouted. He was truly in his element, peeling out of the parking lot in his Firebird while blasting music from the open windows.

"So tell me, who is this we're listening to?" Probably unique among the population at my school, I didn't really care about music. It just wasn't important in my life, or in my house. I don't think I'd ever heard either of my parents with the car radio tuned to music. They liked talk radio, the more conservative the better; I prefer silence when I drive so I can fully concentrate.

"You're kidding, right? This is the Boss, Bruce Springsteen! This song is called 'Badlands.' It was released in 1978. It is the first song on *Darkness on the Edge of Town*."

With that, Paul turned the volume up again and seemed almost in a trance, listening to the music while pushing the Firebird up to seventy when we merged onto the interstate. I was in awe of the passion in his voice as he sang along. I liked to read. I liked lots of things, but they were hobbies; I could tell from his tone that this was an obsession. "So, what's your wheels?"

"Excuse me?" I answered, unsure of the question.

"When you do drive, what kind of car?"

"When I have to drive, my mom lets me use her Jeep."

"That's a weak ride. Does it get you where you want to go, and does it get you there fast?"

"I don't drive fast."

"And you don't listen to the Boss?"

"Only when I've been in this car with you."

"What *do* you do then?" He kind of laughed when he said it, that smirk reappearing. He was almost daring me to come back on him.

Humility wasn't getting me anywhere. "I do just about whatever I want."

"You don't take any crap, do you? I like that," he said.

"Thanks, I think." My nerves were a wreck. It was exhausting trying to keep up with him and act like a more confident person than I really was. I don't know why I lied to him because I rarely did whatever I wanted, mostly because I never really knew what I wanted. Until now.

"You gotta be that way, not take people's crap. If you're a little bit odd, that is what people give you plenty of. Don't take it; you got to throw it back in their stinking faces."

"Technically speaking, their faces would probably not be stinky until it was actually thrown in their faces," I said. And he laughed. I made him laugh, which made me feel great.

"If you act just a little bit strange, everybody wants to grind you down," he said as he bounced his fist off of the steering wheel. "Why am I talking about this with you? You are the honor roll, straight-A, straight-arrow type. What would you know about it?"

"When I first came to school here and didn't have any friends, I used to hide out in the school library before classes and during lunch." My stomach hurt as I had a muscle memory of those early, hard days at school, but I pressed on. "I just really like to read and didn't care about sitting at a table and being ignored, so I know people in school thought I was a weirdo."

"Tell me about it." Paul said, and then laughed. "Like last year in English, we were talking about *Hamlet*. I told Mr. Brown that the real title of the play was *Omelet* and that the first version of the speech was 'two eggs or not two eggs, that is the frying pan.'"

"That's corny," I said with a laugh.

"The whole play is about breakfast: He's Danish; he tells Ophelia, 'Get thee to a bakery.'"

"Too funny."

"You think so? Brown Cow didn't think so," Paul remarked.

"Teachers aren't known for their sense of humor."

"For sure, did you see the way that mofo Mr. Edwards was looking at me at the student council meeting yesterday?" Paul asked.

"What do you mean?" I replied, knowing I couldn't tell Paul that I had watched him just about every minute of the meeting. That rather than listening to the meeting, I was working out last-minute details of my plan to be alone with him. That rather than taking notes for the story I was supposed to write for the newspaper, I was writing out what I would say to him in the car.

"Edwards has it in for me. He doesn't want me on student council."

"Why is that?" I asked.

"He didn't like my campaign slogan last year: Apathy Rules! My thinking was that no one cares about student apathy. People are, you might say, apathetic about apathy."

"So that's why you ran for office?" I asked.

"Look, it was a joke. Brad put me up to it. He told me that I hadn't done anything for three years of school. No sports, no clubs, nothing; so in the yearbook there would be just my senior picture and white space. He sort of dared me. I ran against all those people who cared and I didn't, so it was too funny when I won. I ran against a stoner, a prep, and a jock; so I guess all those votes canceled each other out. I mean, the jocks hate the preps and the stoners hate everybody and everybody hates them. I'm not a part of any of those groups. I'm just a regular guy."

"A guy who doesn't care."

"Right, you're catching on. I got the apathy vote, so the people who don't care are my people. If I'm to represent their interests, then I have to just not care. By not caring, I am showing I care about the things they care about, or in this case, don't care about."

I suddenly noticed my exit whiz past us at seventy-five miles per hour. "Paul, I'm sorry, but do you know where you're going?"

"I guess I got lost." He then turned to look at me, and smiled. "Lost in conversation."

I tried to hold it back, but the blush wouldn't be denied. If your own body won't let you keep secrets, then who can you trust? He moved his right hand, which he had been expertly hiding most of the trip, and put it down very close to the edge of my seat.

I gently touched the top of his hand. Although the do-rag was wrapped around all of it, the damage looked the worst around the knuckles. "Are you okay?"

"My hand? It's nothing," he said. "I had to change a tire on the Firebird and cut it up pretty bad."

"Do you need stitches?"

"No, I'll just buy some superglue," he said, and cranked the volume up one more notch. I sensed that Paul had heard these songs so many times they were practically part of him. "I hope it is the worst thing that happens this year. Lots of pressure in your senior year, you know?"

"I guess," I said weakly. Although I was just a junior, I knew a little bit about pressure.

"Did you have to read that poem 'Rime of the Ancient Mariner' in English class yet?" he said as his voice grew more serious.

"Sure." We hadn't studied that poem in school yet, but I'd read it on my own when I got on this poetry-reading kick last summer.

"I hated most of the stuff they make us read, but I got into that one. The whole thing about the albatross. I think that's what people's expectations are—just a big albatross hanging around your neck that you can't get rid of."

"That's real interesting reading."

"Hell, I don't know why I am telling you this."

I took a deep breath. "I feel the same."

"What? I bet you are like little Miss Responsible. You do what you should."

"That word *should* is my albatross. All I ever hear from my parents is 'Johanna, you should do this.'"

"No doubt, followed by the equally famous: 'Johanna, you shouldn't do that.'"

"I could just scream," I said.

"Then do it!" he said, bouncing his hand off my leg.

"What?"

"Look, all day, every day, we do things people tell us we should do. And we always get told at school to be quiet. I say to hell with that. Let's make some noise."

While Springsteen wailed on in the background Paul shouted out the words and I just screamed. I was surprised we didn't blow our vocal cords out. I imagined what we must have looked like to anyone passing us on the interstate, two people screaming at the top of their lungs. They would have thought us lunatics, and they might just have been right. Somewhere in the middle of the song, screams turned to laughter. I'm not sure what we were laughing at, but it got so bad that Paul had to take an exit to get us off the interstate. At the top of the ramp, we took a second to get it together. He turned the volume down; our laughter was the only sound in the car.

"Hey, where are we?" I asked, jolted back into reality when the car came to a stop.

"I guess I missed the exit. I'll turn around here, or we could just keep driving. I got a full tank of gas and a lot of Springsteen songs I bet you've never heard."

I was blushing again. "Paul, I—"

"Look, about the other day," he said. Although hidden, yesterday had been hanging over both of us: No amount of confessing, laughing, or even screaming was taking that dark cloud away. "I'm sorry about that. Give me a chance to make it up to you. Why don't you come with me tonight to this party at Jackie's house?"

I paused. I wanted to say yes instantly, but I was imagining the scene with my parents. Pam was always trying to get us to go to parties, but my parents kept me on a pretty tight leash.

Paul smiled. "I was gonna take Vickie and—crap, I'm sorry, just never mind."

He was trying to swallow the words back as he picked away at a hole in the green fatigues he was wearing, which I noticed for the first time also had some bloodstains on them. It was a mess: Everything was wrong about this. Everything was wrong in the details, but it was also exactly what I wanted. I swallowed hard, but the words came easy. "I would love to go."

Paul took his injured right hand and put it under my chin.

"So, Johanna, is it too late to change my answer to your question?" Paul asked as he leaned toward me and brought his lips against mine.

EIGHT

"You said you'd go?" Pam didn't sound happy. She was still upset with me for abandoning her at school. I can't say that I blamed her for that.

"It was the right thing to do," I said, cradling the phone on my shoulder as I finished putting on my favorite pair of earrings. It was also my only pair of earrings, since despite my mother's constant coaching, I was such a fashion idiot.

"You let him put you down, then you go out with him? You reward him for making you feel bad?" Pam's interrogative style reminded me of my mother sometimes, although Mom had it down to a cold science. "Books, I don't understand you sometimes."

"That's behind me, Pam. That was a mistake," I said in the calmest tone possible as I looked through the little bit of makeup I owned, trying to figure out how to use any of it. It wasn't something I had a lot of experience with and was yet another case where being smart didn't seem to matter. I looked in the mirror, something I rarely enjoyed doing.

Surrounding my face in the mirror, like some sort of halo, are the report cards my parents put there: the A's lined up in a perfect formation, just as expected. Everywhere I look I see some evidence: There is a best science project certificate from eighth grade; there is a math project award from last year. So if I am so smart, if out of the corner of my eye I can see my 4.0 from sophomore year, why can't I figure out how to apply eyeliner so I don't look like a raccoon?

"Look, Pam, I've really got to get dressed." I had already tried on about twenty different outfits, but I looked hideous and fat in all of them. I finally decided I'd wear a simple black T-shirt and a pair of jeans. I had never seen Paul wear anything but T-shirts and jeans or fatigues, so I thought it was a safe call. I'd throw on my long coat before I went downstairs so I didn't have to hear the expected criticism from my mother about my lack of fashion sense.

"Why bother getting dressed? He's going to spend the night trying to get you undressed."

"Pam, why do you say things like that?" I asked.

"Johanna, why are you so naive?" Pam countered.

I was burning now. Friends, more than enemies, really know how to wound you. "It's not like that."

"Don't kid yourself, Books."

"Pam, listen, please don't talk this way. I'm so sorry about today. Tomorrow we'll go to the bookstore, hang out all afternoon, just like always." Pam and I hung out at school, shared a locker, drove in together, worked on the newspaper, went to movies, IM'd, talked on the phone all the time; but our friendship centered on trips every Saturday to our local bookstore to look for new trashy reads; drink stupidly expensive, fattening beverages; and discuss our little parts of the world.

"Fine. I'm sorry, Books. I just don't want to see you get hurt again," Pam said.

"Look, we'll talk all about it tomorrow, okay?"

"Okay, Books. You go have a great time, and don't do something that I hope to do some day." Pam laughed as she hung up the phone.

I got up off the bed and slipped on my shoes. I couldn't catch a minute to relax, but I was used to it—being hauled every day after school to some lesson or to Girl Scouts or some other event. Constant motion was my normal state. Sometimes I think that my parents believe that if I slow down for a second, I'll stop all together. They are true believers in the laws of inertia.

As I applied just a little bit of lipstick I had a muscle memory. As I pressed the lipstick on, my mouth could almost feel again the kisses Paul and I shared that afternoon. As I started toward the stairs I wasn't thinking about today, but what would happen tonight. Where was the crystal ball? Maybe creating one could be my entry in the district's science olympics.

The sound of the front-door chime never sounded so loud.

"JoJo, get down here!" My father's unmistakable bellow roared up the stairs. Judging the level of impatience in my father's voice was an art I had been practicing since a very young age. I quickly grabbed my long coat, wrapping it tightly around me as I rushed down the stairs.

"The young man's name again." My father rarely asked for information; it was a demand. He was a hard man to refuse: over six feet tall, with a crew cut that was just starting to show a gray touch and a pair of cold, penetrating eyes. He was, for him, in casual attire, meaning he had taken off his tie and replaced his jacket with a sweater. He believes casual-dress days at work are for losers and whiners, two groups he has little affection for in his professional or his personal life. My father isn't all macho, but he respects toughness above all else, even intelligence.

"It's that boy Paul, isn't it, Johanna?" my mother called out.

She was behind me, cigarette in hand and questions at the ready. My mother was also out of her tailored two-piece work getup; but per usual, she looked perfect in jeans and a sweater. Looking at the two of them standing there so emotionally self-confident and physically striking, it was clear to me—despite what the birth certificate, hundreds of baby photos, and the DNA proved as fact—I had to be adopted.

"Yes," I replied. Just before I opened the door, I said a quick silent prayer that my parents wouldn't embarrass me in front of Paul.

Just as Paul stepped inside, my father swept by me with his hand extended. "How do you do, son?"

Paul held his right hand out, which I noticed was by now at least properly bandaged. My father didn't notice as his bear-sized mitt consumed Paul's damaged hand.

"Sorry I'm late." Paul uttered the words pretty well considering the pain he must have been in.

"I didn't notice you were," my father said, looking at his Rolex while releasing what was left of Paul's hand.

"I was late getting off work at the restaurant," Paul said.

"Where is it you work?" The first question, of course, came from my mother. I should have grabbed a chair and waited out the forthcoming nineteen inquiries. I was going to ask Paul to sit down, but it didn't look as if he had changed from work, because the jeans he was wearing were covered with grease stains. I was contemplating the size stroke my mother would have if he sat in any of the perfect chairs in any of the perfect rooms she perfectly agonized over.

I caught the tail end of Paul's answer, and then tried to move us toward the door.

"Did Jo tell you that her grandfather owned a restaurant in Chicago?" my father asked.

Paul shook his head. He didn't know anything about my parents, and I hadn't told them much about Paul, other than he was a member of the student council. I neglected to mention he won on the apathy platform.

"This was back in Chicago." My father loved to tell stories about growing up in Chicago, working in his father's kitchen by day, studying to be an engineer at night, then joining the marines before going to the University of Michigan to get his masters. These stories were always heavy on life lessons about the value of hard work, family, loyalty, and obedience. I heard these stories often. "Have you ever been to Chicago, son?"

"No, I don't travel much, but I'm planning to go to Stanford for college next year," Paul replied. I'm glad no one was paying attention to me, because my head was exploding. I had not even walked out the door with Paul for my first of what I hoped would be many dates with him when I learned he was going away to school. This couldn't even last a year. Pam was right; I was so naive.

"Well, that is a fine school. The school I went to in Chicago was the one they called the school of hard knocks. Heard of it?" My father loved clichés: They were simple, to the point, and easy to understand. And they didn't invite discussion.

Paul smiled. It didn't look fake, but I didn't know his body language well enough yet. I was weighing in my mind how much of his body language I would learn about later this evening.

"During high school, much like yourself, I had to work hard, but it toughened me. It made me a man." I knew what was coming next, and I wanted to hide. "That and the U.S. Marine

Corps." My father rolled up his sleeve to reveal the marines-logo tattoo on his right arm.

I thought my father was going to make Paul feel his arm and watch him flex his muscles. I had to end this. "Mom, Dad, we have to go now."

"Well, you had better go then," my mother said while glancing at my father's watch. "So we will see you no later than eleven."

"Mom, don't you think—"

My father took a step toward me. "Your mother said eleven." He gave me a short, decisive head bob, furrowing his brow. I called this look "getting the brow beat into me."

"I'll see you when you get home, okay, Johanna?" My mother was making sure I knew she would be there guarding the door and watching the clock. "You kids have a nice time."

With that as our send-off, any time would be nice in comparison. As we walked outside I saw my parents standing together, like a united front. There would be no Hallmark moments taking place at my door. I would leave not knowing of their love or affection but only of how I could disappoint them by returning later than eleven.

Paul went ahead of me and had already opened up the door to the Firebird. When I went to sit down, there was a single red rose on the seat. I picked it up by the stem, which was wrapped in tissue paper; it was so cold and so fresh.

"Paul, this is really nice." I pressed the cold petals up against my blushing, warm face.

"It is as beautiful as you." Paul leaned over, brushed his face up near mine, and whispered, "So, Johanna, what do you think your mother meant by a good time?"

I just rolled my eyes and laughed as Paul peeled out of the

driveway. I imagined my parents standing by the window, shaking their heads in unison, wondering where they went wrong. That thought, and the touch of Paul's hand against mine, made me smile.

"Your parents are suits, right?"

"Suits?" I had never heard the expression before.

"Suits, you know, they work in an office or something."

"My dad is a lead engineer at the Chrysler Tech Center, and my mom is a quality control manager there. So I guess you could say they're suits."

I was lost with why he brought this up until I noticed where Paul had stopped. We were parked in front of a nondescript yellow trailer among a sea of other trailers. The kids at school who live in trailer parks are called trash bags. Whenever we drive by a trailer park, my father says, in what for him passes as a joke, that the reason tornadoes destroy trailer parks is because they have an attraction to welfare mothers, pickup trucks, and white trash. I never thought it was funny.

"Just wait here, please. Listen to this Springsteen song while I'm gone; it's called 'Thunder Road.'" He gave my hand a little squeeze and dashed out of the car.

I didn't know anyone who lived in a trailer. I assumed those were the boys who took shop or the girls who spent most of their days sneaking a joint. I guess I looked down on people like that because it made me feel superior. I was so wrong. I turned the volume down. My head was throbbing with thoughts; it didn't need a bass and drum accompaniment.

I wasn't used to being wrong. My parents expected a lot from me, especially that I not make mistakes. I think they wanted those good grades even more than I did. They wanted me to be sensible, but when Paul touched my hand, it made me feel sexy.

"Screw this!" I suddenly heard Paul yell as the door to the trailer slammed behind him.

"You're not old enough to decide." I heard a woman's voice. Paul was standing on the bottom step, glaring up at the front door.

"You're not young enough to know!" Paul shouted.

"Why do you act this way, Paul? Why do you treat me this way?" the woman's voice shouted. I guess I should have tried not to listen, but I couldn't help myself.

Paul stormed the three steps back up to the front door and ripped it open. I thought the door was going to go flying he jerked it with so much force. He rolled up the sleeves of his ratty black-hooded sweatshirt.

"Do you see any needle marks? Do you?" he shouted, and thrust his arms toward the door. "I don't take drugs. I get okay grades in school. I work. So why don't you and Jesus just leave me the hell alone!" Paul slammed the door shut again and came charging out toward the car. A woman, his mother I presumed, pushed the door open and called out after him.

"Because I love you," she yelled back at him, although there was no anger in her voice.

Paul was looking into the car, but I don't think he saw me. I don't think he saw anything through the rage burning in his eyes. He took a deep breath and then pivoted back toward the door where his mother was standing. "Like that matters or means anything."

I glued my eyes to the floor pretending I didn't witness any of it.

Paul jumped in the car, slamming yet another door. Immediately he put his arms around me and then kissed me. He squeezed me, held me tighter than I could ever imagine one person holding another. He took a deep breath and then spoke. "Everything is gonna be okay."

I ran my hand along his face; his jaw was clenched tight with tension. "Are you sure?"

"Sometimes, my mother . . ." He slammed his fist hard off the steering wheel, then sighed. "Everything is going to be okay."

I didn't have a chance to answer before he pressed his lips against mine again. I could tell that the rage was leaving him; he poured all that bitter hard anger into a tender kiss.

NINE

When Paul and I got near the front door at Jackie's house, I saw Brad standing on the porch. "Glad you could make it!"

"Who's at this mofo?" Paul asked as he slapped Brad on the back.

"The usual suspects," Brad said with a smile. He turned his back toward us and shouted inside. "Hey, Kara, come out and play."

"What do you want, baby?" Kara Stevenson emerged seconds later from the house and gave Brad a big hug.

"Kara, this is Johanna," Brad said.

I shot Kara a little wave. "Kara, sure, I've seen you at school."

"Everybody sees Kara," Paul said, slapping Brad's shoulder again. "Some of us see more of Kara than others, isn't that right brother Bradley?"

Kara Stevenson was the center of attention. I don't know how she got her clothes to fit as close to her body as she did, and I was taking honors physics. She seemed to be defying three or four of Newton's laws. She looked vacuum-packed in her black leather dress, amplified by long black boots and purple fishnets. She had a supershort haircut and purple highlights. I not only didn't look anything like her, compared to Kara I felt like I belonged to a different gender. When she wasn't hanging on Brad, she hung out with Lynne and Jackie. The three of them were airheaded model wannabes who worked at trendy clothing stores at the mall.

"Let's find some brew," Paul said, tugging hard on my arm and moving us toward the door. I didn't say anything, stunned that he was trying to drag me like some deadweight. He must have noticed, because he let go when I "laid the brow" on him.

"Sorry about that," Paul said, coughing and laughing at the same time. "Do you want to come inside?"

"If you're asking, then I'm accepting," I said with a smile, yet failing to reach the level of sarcasm I was seeking.

"I may get a cavity being around something so sweet," Brad said, and he turned to go inside with us.

Kara narrowed her eyes; it seemed like she was all purple eye shadow. "Kind of nice to see two people be nice to each other," she said as she walked out toward the street.

"Ouch!" Paul said, smacking the back of his hand off of Brad's chest.

"Kara, baby, come back!" Brad said following after her.

"Did I—" I started.

"No, just the same old bull," Paul said. "They fight, they breakup, they get back together, blah, yadda, blah."

I shook my head, then sighed. "Doesn't sound too smart to me."

"It works for them," Paul said with a shrug of his shoulders. He took a step toward the door, letting his right hand hang behind, dangling it in front of me like bait. I took it. I reached my left hand out and let him grab on to it, then we walked in the front door.

Once inside, the music hit us. It was pretty dark, dotted by the ends of lit cigarettes. People were milling around; almost everywhere small groups had formed. We walked down the hall, through a couple of rooms, then downstairs. Paul found the keg in the laundry room. He quickly filled up a big red plastic cup with beer and offered it to me.

"No, thanks," I said, accenting it with small head shakes. Paul shrugged his shoulders, downed the beer in two giant gulps, then tossed the cup onto the floor.

"Now, young lady, I just said you should have a good time, didn't I?" Paul was doing my mother's voice.

"Stop, okay? I got the point." I was laughing too hard for jeans as tight as the ones I was wearing.

"Drinking is what made me a man." Paul rolled up the sleeve on his right arm. He grabbed both of my hands and put them on his bicep. He puffed out his chest and started banging on it like Tarzan. "That and the U.S. Marines! Don't you want to be a man, soldier?"

I started to cry I was laughing so much. While I was out of commission Paul took the opportunity to grab another cup, down the contents, and then fill it for the third time.

The music-filled room was almost totally dark. From what I could see, people were mostly just holding on to each other, shuffling their feet and locking lips.

Paul set his beer on a table, then took a few steps away from me, out toward the part of the basement doubling as a dance floor. He stretched his hand out before him. "Climb in?"

I hid my eyes and moved closer. He pulled me tighter, his arm snug around my waist. He had to put his mouth right next to my ear to be heard.

"Sure," I barely managed to squeak out. Paul moved his right arm tighter and lower around me, while his left arm went around my back. We were moving in small circles. With each beat of the song, we drew the circle smaller, closer, tighter. I was glad the music was loud, so Paul couldn't hear me gasping for breath; although I realized as tight as he was holding me, he had to feel it.

We danced for a long time, taking breaks for Paul to crack a joke or two with groups of seniors who would pass by; then we would go back to dancing. Finally I stole a glance at my watch and noticed that it was almost eleven. "Paul, I need to go now."

"Sure, no problem," he said, leading me by the hand through the darkness and up the stairs. But rather than heading outside, Paul kept walking up another flight of stairs. He was almost pulling me, but I wasn't pulling back as he opened the door to a small bedroom.

The room was small and dark. I could make out the outlines of posters on the wall and of a small bed. Paul locked the door behind us, then led me by the hand over toward the bed; but about a foot away I stopped him.

"Yes or no?" Paul asked. I buried my head in his shoulder. I didn't want Paul to see my eyes. Everything seemed to be moving so fast, spinning out of control. I was used to controlling things, keeping everything organized; but I felt it all slipping away from me. I was thinking how the other night I was lying in my bed crying about Paul, thinking about all those nights, weeks, and months before, there all alone just thinking about him. Now here I was in some stranger's bedroom, those thoughts coming true like I had been looking into a crystal ball.

"What's wrong?" Paul said as he pressed both my hands against his chest. "I thought—"

I kissed him. Kissing I had done; kissing I knew how to do. That had always been the cutoff with Ty, but then he cut me off.

Part of my brain was wondering what I was doing here; the other part remembered that I had spent more time deciding what to wear under my clothes than anything else.

Paul moved around behind me, putting his arms around my waist. We were looking through the darkness straight down at the bed in front of us.

"I'm sorry I was late. I promise it won't happen again," Paul said as he rubbed his thumb gently along the side of my face. "That is, if you want me to pick you up again."

His voice was tentative. Was he as scared as I was? I couldn't imagine it. I knew he had gone out with a girl from South High named Carla; I managed to get that information from Brad. I assumed he had lots of girlfriends before her. He seemed so confident; that was part of the attraction. I seemed that way, too, when it came to knowing the answer to a math problem, but inside I was really a mess. And with boys I was hopeless. Could he just be acting, too?

"Paul, I—"

"Tonight is too short. If only it wasn't so late. It's because of that damn lousy job. That's why I had a few beers, you know. I'm not like that, but it helps me relax. That job gets my body so sore sometimes, especially my back."

"Your back?"

"I work as a dishwasher at Wallies. And if I can't get the dishes clean, I just break them and then throw them in the trash. Not all of them, just the real dirty ones I don't want to deal with. Then as long as I take the trash out, nobody seems to know, although it sure makes the trash bags heavy, which is hell on my back."

"The old smash 'em and trash 'em," I said. I was trying to be funny because I didn't know what else to say. I never had a job outside of the house, which was more my parent's choice than mine, but I knew that my father would have recommended me for a lifetime grounding if he caught me taking a shortcut like that. Maybe it is different for people who weren't raised in a house run by the captains of quality control.

"My back hurts a lot." Paul walked past me and took those huge steps toward the bed. He lay facedown on the bed. He turned his head and looked up at me. Even in the near darkness I could still see his smile. "It hurts a lot, and all that dancing sure didn't help."

I didn't say anything. The room was totally silent. There was still noise from the party going on outside, but I had shut the rest of the world out.

"Would you like me to rub your back?" I asked in a voice so small I was hoping he wouldn't hear.

"Would you?" Paul responded.

I sat down on the bed next to him. I had seen people do this at school. Last year a big back-rubbing craze took over until the teachers put an end to it. It seemed like such an obvious thing to do, but I'd never taken part in it. I started moving my hands around his shoulders, hoping I wasn't hurting him. I was such a klutz; I couldn't believe I was doing this. He would probably walk out of this room in a body cast.

"That's nice," Paul said, not even looking up. He let out a low moan. "Really nice."

I just kept my hands moving, working my way down his back. I made small rubbing circles, like those small circles we had danced earlier tonight. My hands were remembering the pressure of his body up against me. Pressure: I had always thought of that word as a negative thing, but as my hands pushed down against the surface of Paul's back I realized that pressure could be a good thing.

"Thanks, that was great," Paul said, rotating over to face me. "Your turn."

"But my back doesn't hurt," I meekly protested.

"Well, if your back doesn't hurt, then this won't hurt either." I moved next to him on the bed, but Paul tried to pull me on top of him.

"Everything is going to be okay. Trust me," Paul said, taking his glasses off and setting them on a table next to the bed.

I looked at him, and I believed. Believed everything was going to be all right. Believed in him as I let him pull me down and we started kissing. His hands were moving up my back, then along the side of my face. Paul's tongue and teeth were working around my ear. It felt so nice, but then I felt a slight pull on my lobe. My earring! I heard it hit the floor.

"Paul, wait." I reached a hand down toward the floor.

"Let it go," Paul said, then started kissing me again as his hands started moving over me. I was kissing him with passion, but I wasn't all there. I couldn't shut my blasted mind down and just let the pleasure I was feeling take over. Moving against Paul in the darkness, our bodies grinding away at each other, I was thinking how sex wasn't just a simple matter of answering no. It was about deciding why, when, where, how, and with whom. I was thinking I had answered that last question first.

"Ah, crap, no." I heard Paul let out a huge sigh, then he quickly moved off of me and over to the door. "We'd better get going."

I glanced at my watch. It was almost one A.M. My parents probably had the police looking for me. "My mother is going to kill me."

"What about your father?"

"He'll kill you!"

"Great, just great," Paul said as he started to open the door.

"Where's my earring?" I asked him as my eyes tried to adjust to the darkness and find a light switch. "I need to turn the light on."

"No! Don't turn on the light," Paul said. He reached to the floor and picked up his sweatshirt, quickly wrapping it around his waist like an apron. I gathered up my coat and chased Paul as he took off in a mad dash for the Firebird. I was just about out the door when I bumped into Brad and Kara standing hand in hand on the porch.

"Did Paul run by here?" I asked.

"Your Paul is really something, isn't he?" Brad said, sidling over to me.

"He sure is," I replied, fascinated with Brad's choice of words. He'd said "your." Your was the possessive pronoun. Brad was right; Paul was "really something." The main thing that he was now, however, was mine.

We listened to Springsteen all the way home, with Paul introducing each song. I fell in love with the song "If I Should Fall Behind" immediately. When we finally pulled into my driveway, the lights in the house were still on. Paul gave me a quick good night kiss, and I ran toward the door.

I didn't even get the key in the lock before my mother opened the door. "What do you have to say for yourself, young lady?"

"I'm sorry." I could barely speak.

"Your father went to bed. Do you know how lucky you are he's not here?" My mom's eyes were manic. "What should we say to him?"

I didn't even look up. "That I'm sorry."

"I don't think that is enough of an answer, do you?" my mother said, raising her voice. "Go to your room. We'll discuss this more in the morning. You should be ashamed of yourself."

That was too much. I felt bad being late, but I was not ashamed. "I have nothing to be ashamed of."

My mother looked surprised; she was not used to anything but silent obedience, yet something about all the emotion of the evening just stirred defiance within me. "You're wrong. Would you mind telling me when your curfew was? Are you suddenly not smart enough to tell time?"

"It's not that simple, Mom." All I could feel was her anger and her disappointment, when all I wanted was her understanding.

"Yes, it is that simple." She was staring at me now. I knew she could see my lipstick was smeared from kissing. I am sure she noticed that my clothes were rumpled. I am sure she locked on to the fact that one of my earrings was missing. I knew she could tell that despite all of this, despite this terrible scene, deep inside I was smiling.

"Johanna Marie, you know right from wrong. Your father and I taught you right from wrong. This is wrong, isn't it?"

I said nothing.

"Isn't it?"

I started walking up the stairs, away from all of this. My mother's declarations of right and wrong seemed meaningless. I wanted to ask her how she got this way. I wanted to ask her how she got to be this controlling. She was a smart woman; she had to know this wasn't the right way to speak to me. She knew right from wrong, too.

"What do you think this type of behavior is going to get you?" she loudly asked.

I just looked at her and started walking up the stairs. Over my shoulder I saw the smoke from her cigarette, and I thought about the fire I felt for Paul. *What is this going to get me? Exactly what I want,* I thought as I walked silently into my room and toward a peaceful sleep.

TEN

I sat down on the front steps of the Pontiac Main Library. My early morning arrival led my parents to ground me, including my normal visit to the bookstore with Pam on Saturday. I finally managed to get out of the house on Sunday by proclaiming the need, real if slightly exaggerated, to do research at the library. Playing the study card, I had learned, always worked with my parents. As I sat outside feeling a cool September breeze I thought how I should have taken that back rub from Paul the other night: lugging around this bag full of textbooks hurt. I put my book bag down, pulled out *Jane Eyre* again, and started to read.

I got maybe thirty pages knocked off when I heard the Firebird roar up in front of the library. Paul slammed the brakes to bring the car to a squealing halt. He jumped from the car and scampered up the steps like a madman, grabbed my bag, then raced back down the stairs. He opened the passenger door in a broad sweeping gesture, then tossed my bag into the backseat. "Ms. Eyre, your carriage waits, so climb in!"

I laughed, and he snatched my hand and walked us hurriedly toward the car. "We have less than an hour, and I know a great place we can go."

I shot him the brow. "A great place for what?"

"For this," Paul said, pulling me toward him. We kissed, just like the other night. Our lips seem to work well together. I stopped, moved away for a second, and smiled before kissing him back. I wanted him to see how happy I was.

I sat down in the passenger seat, only to feel something underneath me. I inched up in the seat and pulled out a small package. "What's this?"

Paul didn't say anything. He slammed the car into drive, and we took off for parts unknown.

I tore open the gift wrap. I couldn't ever remember getting a gift from Ty, or from anyone other than a member of my family. Sometimes I thought I knew so much, but then times like this, I realized how much I hadn't experienced. I opened the box.

"Paul!" I said as I pulled the star-shaped earrings from the box. "They're beautiful."

"You're what's beautiful. If the earring fits," he said, adding a laugh as punctuation.

I turned the car's rearview mirror toward me. I put the earrings on and couldn't believe how wonderful they looked, but mostly I couldn't believe how I looked. I actually looked pretty. I had to get glasses at a really young age, so I always kind of looked goofy as a kid. Boys at school would make fun of me, call me ugly. I don't think at eight or ten years old I had the capacity to realize it was just kids being stupid; instead, I believed them. Then when I got to junior high, I grew taller faster than a lot of the boys, so they made fun of me again. I had braces. I was such a squirrel. No wonder I spent all my time hiding in the library, reading. By the time I got to high school, I couldn't imagine thinking that I was pretty in a world full of Karas and Vickies. There was just nothing remarkable about me. My breasts, my butt, my height, my weight, everything—just normal. Looking into the mirror with Paul next to me and seeing myself in my new earrings, I felt special. It didn't matter if I was beautiful, just that Paul thought I was.

I was so caught up in my thoughts, I barely noticed that Paul had slowed the car down. We were in an area downriver in the shadow of the interstate and a closed-down auto factory.

"Where are we?"

"That's the old assembly plant. My grandfather used to work there, but nobody works there anymore. It's nice and quiet and deserted." Paul was inching over closer to me. He moved closer to me, slipping his left hand underneath my jacket. He took his right hand and put it behind my neck. His left hand was working its way up the side of my body. My lips were pressing against his while my hand was gently pushing his away.

"What's wrong?" he whispered. "Why can't I touch you?"

"You are touching me," I said softly. "Kissing is touching, holding is touching, hugging is touching. Let's go slow, okay?"

Paul moved his left hand away and slammed it hard off the steering wheel. He sat there for a minute; I could see the activity going on behind his eyes.

"I didn't mean to make you angry," I said softly. I was looking at him, trying to figure things out. What is the difference? When is it groping, and when is it touching? Was it okay to do these things if you called someone your boyfriend? I'd been down this road once before, with Ty. I thought he liked me, but I soon saw what he wanted from me. Maybe if my Dad saw me with Ty, he might have appreciated how tough I could be. "I just don't want to be rushed again."

"Again? It sounds like you speak from experience." There was an angry and jealous tone in his voice.

"You should talk; I know all about you and Carla." I knew it

was a mistake the minute it was out of my mouth. Was I this ju-
venile? This jealous? The earth should open up and swallow anyone as stupid as me.

He took a deep breath. "There's not much to know. It just
didn't work out."

"That's not what I heard." I really hadn't heard anything, but
I was dying to know and too afraid to ask him directly.

"What did you hear?" he came right back at me.

"Brad told me about the two of you." That wasn't exactly true.
Brad had only told me that she went to South High.

"Let's change the subject. I never ever want to hear that name
again," he said sharply.

"Paul, is there something wrong?" The bounce had vanished
from his voice.

"No, I just don't want to talk about it." He eyes were glued to
the floor, and he was biting his bottom lip.

"Paul, is there something about Carla you want to tell me?
Are you hiding something?" I thought that I had a pretty good
sense of when people were lying to me. Paul leaned toward me;
his forehead was resting against mine. I could hear his words, but
I couldn't see his eyes.

"Trust me." He kissed his own fingers, then put them over
my lips. "Now you're the next contestant on true romance con-
fessions."

"His name was Ty. It was over last May."

"How long did you go out? What was he like?"

I shifted uncomfortably in the seat. I started picking at the
upholstery. "We only went out for a couple of months. We had
nothing in common. He was just somebody I knew from the
neighborhood. My parents didn't like him."

"Not like they love me."

I laughed. "Anyway, they couldn't stand him, and I guess after a while he didn't like me too much, either." I was revealing far more than I wanted. Maybe we should have just kept making out. This was a lot more intimate and personal and embarrassing than Paul sliding his hand underneath my T-shirt.

"Well, I'm not the smartest guy in the world," Paul said, leaning in toward me again. He took his hand, rubbing it softly against my lips, then the side of my face. "But at least I'm not as stupid as Ty. You are wonderful. He's an idiot not to want to be with you."

"I was thinking the same about Carla."

"Let's promise, then, that we won't talk about those losers again, because we're pulling out of here to win," Paul whispered.

"Promise," I said. Who needed the past when I had in Paul a wonderful present.

"You know, I thought Pam was your boyfriend," Paul said with a grin.

"What?" I must not have heard him right. "Pam is my best friend."

"She's a dyke, you know that, right?" Paul said, making it sound like it was well-known.

"Pam isn't gay!" I said with great confidence. "Who told you that?"

"That's what everybody thinks. So if you're spending time with her, people think you're gay, too. That's why I didn't kiss you right away. I thought you were like her, but I guess I was wrong about that," he said, leaning in toward me.

"You're wrong about Pam," I insisted. Pam and I were best friends; she couldn't keep something like that secret from me.

We told each other everything. Paul was just wrong, but I could tell his mind was made up.

"I think you shouldn't hang out with her anymore," Paul said, then pulled me toward him. "I think you'll find time with me a lot more fulfilling, if you know what I mean."

He laughed, then turned up the music. Even as we started kissing again, I was hoping the heat in my face would dry up the tears welling behind my eyes. I could taste these tears. It was a flavor, a very sweet flavor, that I had never tasted before, but I knew. I knew. My waiting and wanting was over.

ELEVEN

Dear Dead Dad:
It's Paul, again.

I am sitting here with you all around me.

I guess it's been about a month, all the way since September, since I've been here at room 127 of the Atlas Mini-Storage. I started seeing that girl Johanna. I spent three solid years wanting Vickie, three years smashing my head into a wall of rejection. I decided, like with Carla, if I couldn't get what I wanted, I would start getting what I needed.

You notice I don't come here much anymore. After work I'll go home and call Johanna or send her an E-mail. I pick her up first thing in the morning, and we drive into school together. She is the last person I talk to before I go to bed. When I am in school, I look for her. I smile just knowing her. We spent last Saturday afternoon just driving around in the Bird, listening to the Boss, and laughing. There is no fear. I can't explain it, maybe because I don't understand it. I don't understand any of it, but I never understood anything that happened with Carla, either.

I first saw Carla about a year ago when I was
taking the SATs in my junior year. That, and the
fact I didn't study anything much the night before—
except the ingredients listed on the Stroh's
bottle—explained why I tanked them. I had to work
the first go-around, so I had to go over to South
High to take the test. If I was going to go to Stanford with Brad, I had to do well. So, there I was,
and I saw her, two rows over. She was tall; she was
gorgeous. Not like Vickie, no one was like Vickie,
but something special. She had this crazy red hair:
It looked like her head was sprouting oranges. She
was wearing a black leather jacket, dark blue jeans,
and a white T-shirt. I couldn't take my eyes off
her, even as they handed out the test and went over
the instructions. Once the test started, I would
read a question, tell myself, okay, you are not
going to look up at her. Buckle down and answer the
question, but I couldn't control myself. Every time,
my eyes wandered over to her. She was concentrating
so hard, putting her pencil in her mouth, trying to
suck the right answers out. I lost it. She got done
well before me. She wasn't the first to hand in her
test, but she got done pretty quickly. She was going
to hand in that test, leave the room, and I would
never see her again.

I had to decide.

It took just a second. I got up and handed in
my test with about 75 percent of it complete and
followed her out of the classroom. She was bundling
herself up in her jacket and putting on a long black

scarf. She had stepped outside, and I decided to
make my move. I was tired, a little hungover, and
pissed off at myself. It was enough of a combination
to hurl me over fears of rejection and take a risk.
I had nothing to lose.

"Hey, was that some test or what?" I tapped her on the shoulder
to get her attention.

"Sure." She looked confused, but not upset.

"I think SAT stands for Staring at Time."

"Maybe." She smiled, but didn't laugh.

"Or maybe Seeking Another Thought, or maybe Shit! Another Test!"

She laughed. Sometimes you had to go right to the blue material. "Hi, I'm Paul."

"Carla." I waited, and she finally responded, putting out her hand. I took a quick look to make sure there was no class ring branding those long, lovely fingers.

"I go to Pontiac West," I said, a little more confident now.

"I figured. I don't remember seeing you."

"I would certainly remember seeing you." I threw a Hail Mary pass; it was now or never. "Hell, a blind man would remember seeing you."

She laughed, putting her hand over the top of her mouth, ending her performance with a small eye roll. "Oh, that's funny."

"Really? That's kind of my calling card." I shoved my hands in my pockets so she wouldn't see them shaking. "Actually Sprint is my calling card, although I have been known, despite repeated advice to the contrary, to dial 0 rather than 1-800-Collect."

She didn't say anything, only flashed a nice smile. I took that as a good sign.

"I'm so tired. I was up all night studying." It wasn't true, but she didn't need to know that.

"I know, me, too," she said, then yawned.

"Do you wanna get some coffee?" I pushed my foot out in front of me, rubbing my toe across an imaginary line. I was channeling Brad; no way I could do this alone.

She hesitated for a minute, looking at the ground in front of her. I had blown it, so I forged ahead. Nothing left to lose. "Your boyfriend is probably coming to pick you up, probably after he's done with football practice where he bounces linemen off the ground like they had Superballs in their butts."

"He doesn't play football."

"Then I'm not scared of him, so will you have a coffee with me?" I saw her blush; she kind of shrugged her shoulders. "We need to recover from the SAT: Students Accepting Tension. Maybe SAT stands for Smart-Ass Trial." She laughed and followed me out to the Bird.

"You are too funny," she said. And she smiled; that smile was all I ever needed.

I was having a good morning. I had cracked her up a couple of times, almost getting her to spit her caffe latte through her nose. Turned out her boyfriend was a basketball player. She waited until we were sitting at Starbucks to tell me.

"But maybe we can be friends." I let it go for a second. She didn't know what a trigger that was for me. She didn't know the many different ways Vickie had said that to me. I just sat there blowing the heat off my coffee, which made sense as Carla had just blown all the heat out of me. We sat in silence for a bit, then

I stood up and walked away from the table. I refilled my coffee, then stopped by the coffee bar. I grabbed a pitcher of cream and a few packets of sugar, then returned to the table.

"Well, Carla, let me tell you something." I pushed my black coffee into the middle of the table. "I'll drink my coffee black, but I would like it better with cream and sugar."

She just looked at me, again with the small head shakes. "What do you mean?"

"Look, I don't know you, so I don't have anything to lose here." I poured cream and sugar into my coffee, then mixed them together. "Coffee is good, but it's better like this. If you want, we can be friends. That is fine with me. But I think we could be better than that."

"Paul," she said, but I couldn't read her tone. She looked a little shocked, a little confused; but mostly, it seemed, she looked interested. She didn't slap my face, and she didn't leave the table. She just kind of sat there, taking it all in, waiting for me to make the next move.

I took a deep breath, imagined what Brad would do, and then took a pen out of my pocket. "Carla, I enjoyed meeting you. I even enjoyed maybe failing the SAT because I cared more about looking over at the shape of your beautiful face than figuring out square roots. I'm sorry you just want to be friends, but if you change your mind . . ." I scratched out my E-mail address on a napkin and pushed it over to her. I hoped she didn't notice my hand was shaking, and it wasn't just from the coffee working its magic on me.

I didn't even look back as I walked out the door.

When I got the E-mail from Carla on Tuesday morning, Dad, I couldn't believe it. She told her boyfriend about me on Saturday, they broke up on Sunday, she missed school on Monday, then E-mailed on Tuesday. I E-mailed her back, and we got together right away. We started spending all of our time together and became consumed with each other. Turned out, she had had lots of boyfriends, which intimidated me. But then I figured I could learn from their mistakes, which was something I had never been too good at.

I didn't even want to go to my stupid junior prom, but she insisted. It was our worst fight ever. Before that day in May, we would break up, get back together, fight some more, and then she would try to end it; but I wouldn't let her leave me. After the prom we were making out and I was pushing myself on top of her, but she kept shoving me off. I decided to end it once and for all with a hard smack of the back of my hand across Carla's face a couple of times. That turned out to be the end, but that smack across her face certainly wasn't the first, just the worst.

Nobody knows about this. Brad suspects, but he doesn't know for sure. Johanna will never learn about this, because I'm not going to be that way again. I know Carla. She won't tell anybody, because she doesn't want anyone to know about it either. I have kept this a secret, Dad, and so can you. After all, I've kept your secret all these years. It's the least you can do for me.

TWELVE

I looked at my watch, maybe for the twentieth time in the past ten minutes, as if looking at it would have some effect. I stood waiting on my front porch in the early November cold. I never even invited Paul into the house anymore. My parents had no use for him ever since that first date when I missed my curfew. I could tell they were just waiting until we broke up so they could prove once again that they were right and knew more about how to run my life than I did. They had done everything but forbid me from going out with him, but spend time with him is just what I did the day I got off being grounded last month. Not only did they not like Paul, but I knew they resented how much time I spent with him. Sometimes I thought they were even jealous.

I put my hand over my mouth, stifling a yawn. I was exhausted. Paul and I had talked until past midnight; then when my mother screamed at me to get off the phone, we IM'd for another hour. Paul was now bringing me to and from school every day, and normally we would spend our lunch together in his car or anyplace we could be alone. Instead of eating lunch with Paul today, I took time to get caught up with Pam, since I didn't even see her anymore for our bookstore ritual. Paul had changed his work schedule, so he and I usually spent Saturdays together. I knew Pam was happy for me, but I just couldn't find time to see her anymore.

I looked at my watch again, then chewed on my thumb before sticking my hands in my pockets and out of the cold. *Why can't he be on time?* I thought. *I'm always on time for him, and especially tonight when we are celebrating our two-month anniversary.* I reached up and touched the star-shaped earrings he gave me. I wore them all the time. I didn't take them off for any reason. I started to go for my watch again, but I felt guilty. Paul bought me this great gift and had been so nice to me the past two months. It was silly to be mad just because he was running a little late. It was just a mistake. He always made up for it when he made a mistake.

From a distance I heard that sound I had come to love: the churning sounds of the Boss battling the Firebird's aging muffler for noise rights. The Firebird turned into the driveway, and Paul jumped out of the car.

"Forgive me, my lady fair." He went down on one knee. "I offer only a slight gift as an act of forgiveness."

"Speaking of acting—"

Before I could finish, Paul produced a single red rose. "For thine gift explains and, I hope, forgives my tardy nature."

"Paul." I just shook my head; he was always giving me gifts.

"A rose by any other name is a rose is a rose is a rose, blah, yadda, blah."

"It's beautiful." I leaned over to kiss him on the cheek.

"What's this cheek crap?" Paul said, switching from the accent of a Shakespearean actor to that of a street tough. "Can I get some lip action here or what?"

I stood up, and I gave him a big hug, then the kiss on the lips he had requested. I sensed that maybe my mother was watching me; I must have smelled the smoke in the air, so I held the kiss for a long time. "Can't you be serious?"

"I can be serious any time!" Paul said, holding his finger in the air as if making an important point. "I can be serious any time I'm not being funny."

"Let's go; we're already running late." I gave him another hug and started toward the car. He followed and opened the door for me. "Brad and Kara will think that we've—"

I couldn't finish, because on the seat there were the other eleven roses.

"What? You thought I only sprung for one rose?" He started sniffling and pretending to dry his eyes. "I am deeply hurt. I mean what kind of person do you think I am?"

"A wonderful one," I said, the words choking out of me as I picked the roses up and sat down in my seat in his Firebird.

"I'm really sorry I'm late," Paul said, backing out the driveway slowly. My dad had told me to tell Paul that the next time he left rubber in his driveway, he would be cleaning if off with his tongue. Since then, his exits from my house had become less dramatic.

I put the roses on my lap, then cuddled up next to him. "How was work?"

"It was the best day at work: payday!" He was smiling as he said it. He pulled me closer to him. "I promise you every Thursday when I get paid, I'll buy you something. What is your favorite thing in the entire world—other than me, that is?"

"That's a silly question." I didn't need Paul to buy me gifts. In fact, part of me didn't feel I deserved it. I wasn't as wonderful as he thought I was, and I kept wondering when he was going to figure that out.

"Joha, I'm being serious here," Paul continued. "What could I bring you each week that would make you happy?"

"Well, I really love ice cream." That was putting it mildly. I was once happy to envision thoughts of living my life in my parent's basement, eating ice cream and reading fantasy novels all day until they would come with the forklift to take me to an early, but very happy, grave.

"Ice cream it shall be!" Paul said, snapping his fingers. "There's a Baskin-Robbins just down the street from Santi's Pizza. What flavor?"

"Peanut butter," I said without hesitation.

He frowned for a second. "Got another?"

"Oh." Had I failed some taste test?

"I just hate peanut butter, that's all, and I might want to lick from your cone sometime."

"Paul, you have a way with words, that's for sure." I laughed when I said it, which helped force down the blush I felt overtaking me. "How about chocolate chip then?"

"Okay, but remember if you eat all that ice cream, you'll get fat unless you exercise. Know any physical activity to burn off those calories?" Paul started tickling my stomach as he spoke.

"Stop it!" I said it loudly, but I was laughing. "Hey, where are we going?"

"You're always so serious, Joha. I think I need to loosen you up." He pushed down on the accelerator, and we roared down the road.

Rather than heading toward the interstate, Paul drove in the opposite direction down my street. After a while, he pulled into the parking lot of St. Mary's, the church that my parents and I went to every Sunday. Paul turned the radio and the lights off, then pulled toward the back of the deserted parking lot, in a tree-covered area. He wasn't talking.

"Are you mad at me, Paul?" I asked.

"I'm not mad. I'm a man with a plan, understand?" he said.

"Paul, this is too strange to be here," I said, the tension in my voice obvious to Paul. My parents are pretty religious, and I guess deep down I was, too. I believed what Paul and I had been doing, and what he wanted us to be doing in the future, was wrong. He kept pushing for more of me, and as I was falling deeper in love with him it was getting so much harder to pull back.

He just looked at me, then smiled. He started kissing my neck again, then biting on my ears, and then back to kissing my lips. His mouth was moving all over me, as were his hands.

My glasses were steaming up: In fact, all the windows in the Bird were steaming up. It was like being in a fog. I held Paul close to me, but had to push him away when I felt his hand go under my dress and touch me above my knee.

"Please, Paul, I don't want to—"

He pushed himself away from me, grinding his palm into my shoulder. "Damn it, Johanna." He raised his left fist in the air, slamming it down on his steering wheel, accidentally hitting the horn. "Great, just great."

As the sound of the horn faded we sat there in silence. I reached out to him, stroking his right arm. "Not here, not now." It was all I could manage to say.

"Then when?" he asked softly, stroking my hair. "Then where?"

"I just don't know; I don't know." I was a mess. I could count on one hand all the times I answered "I don't know" at school, but I was setting some sort of record this evening. Honors physics was easy compared to the balancing of the mind with the body and the heart. This was a science I didn't think I would ever understand.

"I want to touch you. Really touch you." Paul turned and looked me right in the eyes. He took my glasses off and set them on the dash.

My vision was bad, but I knew every inch of his face by now. I touched his bottom lip with my finger. "Paul, I just don't know."

"I know I want more. I want all of you."

I think I stopped breathing for a second. I closed my eyes, trying to soak his words into my head. "Paul, I don't mean to be this way. I just don't know if I'm ready."

"Joha, I need you. I'd be lost without you." He was rubbing his hand lightly against my cheek, brushing his fingertips every now and then across my shoulders.

"And I need you," I said softly. I shut my eyes, squeezing them tight as if I could push out the answer I wanted from him to the question I needed to ask. "Paul, do you love me?"

"Of course I do," Paul said, without skipping a beat. He pulled me closer to him.

I was about to cry. I knew if it started, I couldn't stop. "You never told me that before."

"You never asked."

"Paul, I want to make you happy," I said, moving closer to him. "I'm just not ready. I want to be with you. I guess it's wrong, but I don't care about that. But I want it to be beautiful: I want us to be able to spend the night together, not be crunched up here in a car."

He sighed, then put his fingers over my mouth. "It's okay, Joha; we can wait," he said, reaching his hands out in front of him, pulling me back toward him. In the darkness, even without our glasses we could see each other clearly. I could see inside him. I could feel the beating of his heart. I knew it was in perfect time with mine. I just wanted to make him happy, make him feel as happy as I was feeling now.

"I want to Paul, but—"

"Everything is going to be okay. We can wait for that. We're not going anywhere."

"What else should I do to make you feel good?" I asked. He pulled me toward him, putting my hands between his legs. "Tell me what to do, Paul. I don't know."

"Where have you been?" Brad shouted at us when we finally walked into Santi's later that evening. "Paul, I realize you're a senior in high school, so some concepts are behind you; but nine o'clock is when the big hand is on the twelve and the little hand is on the nine."

Paul pointed at me. "She's the math whiz. Tell her about your crazy formulas, not me."

I was wondering what Paul was going to tell them, but I figured the big smile on his face matching the one on mine was probably telling the story without sound. I was also holding the single red rose Paul had given me. I stuck it in the vase on the table and then gave Paul a hug.

Paul grabbed Brad by the shoulders. "Get over there, already," he said, pretending to pull Brad out of the booth. Brad got up and tucked himself into the other side of the booth next to Kara.

"You guys eat yet?" Paul asked as he sat down near the edge of the booth. He grabbed me around the waist and pulled me so I was sitting on his lap.

"Like an hour ago," Kara snapped. Her color of the night was blue, including a thin midnight blue scarf hanging around her shoulders. "Hi, Johanna, how are—"

"My fault!" Paul said, throwing his hands in the air. "I take the blame. In fact, I think I'll have a large order of blame, with a side of sorry and a glass of shame to chase it all down."

He was laughing at his own joke and wrapping his arms around me.

Kara and Brad stood up. Brad put on her coat, then his own. "I got bad news, and I got good news."

Paul put his hand on his chin as if in deep contemplation. "I think I'll take the bad news first, then."

"We're leaving now," Brad said as he held Kara's hand tight. "Well, the good news is more for you, Chief."

"Hit us," Paul said.

"Your buddy Pam was in looking for you. She said she would stop back to see you," Brad said as he and Kara walked away from the table toward the cash register to pay their bill.

"Great, just great." Paul slapped his hands so hard off the table that every head in the restaurant turned to look at us.

"Please, Paul, don't be that way," I said. "Let's invite Pam to join us if she comes back."

"I'm dating you, not your dyke friend," he said as he jabbed his index finger hard into my shoulder.

"I just—"

"Let's blow before she gets here," Paul said, pushing me to get out of the booth.

"Paul, she's my friend," I protested.

"Whatever. Now why don't you start moving your fat ass?" Paul hissed at me. He grabbed both of my wrists and squeezed them hard. I tried to pull away, but he was too strong.

"That hurts," I said, holding back tears. He let go, but then balled his right hand into a fist and rammed it hard against my left wrist.

"Life hurts, Joha. You had better get used to it," Paul said through clenched teeth. He grabbed the rose I'd put in the vase and threw it at me. "Ask Pam to buy you roses, then!"

"Paul, please, she's my friend. I need to—" I didn't finish as he shoved me out of the booth and pushed me aside.

"I thought you said you needed *me*. You lied."

"Paul, please wait!"

He never made eye contact, instead just marched toward the door where Kara and Brad were still standing, watching the scene from a distance. Paul stopped by the door, turned to me, and shouted across the room, "Are you coming or not?"

I started toward Paul, hoping we could somehow make this scene less public. "Just a few minutes, she's my friend."

Paul glared at me. If earlier in the car I thought he could see inside of me, now he was looking right through me. "It's either her or me. You had better decide!" Paul shouted, slamming the door as his exclamation point.

Kara came over, while Brad finished up paying their bill. Before any of us got to the door, I heard the sound of the Firebird screeching off into the night.

"Paul! Paul!" Brad opened the door and ran out onto the sidewalk. We followed behind.

The cold wind bounced against my face like needles. "It's my fault." I was shaking.

"Don't worry, we're not going to leave you here," Brad said, putting his arm around me. I noticed the look that Kara gave him. He must have noticed as well, backing away from me.

I turned to Kara, hoping she could be of some help. "Should I stay and wait for him?"

"I wouldn't." She sounded bored, but then she surprised me by laughing. She pointed her index finger with the nail extended out like a blue sword at Brad, swishing it back and forth and making cutting sounds. "You know what they say. 'Boys will sometimes be boys, but they will almost always be assholes.'"

I didn't laugh; there was nothing funny about this for me. "I didn't mean to make him mad. Why was he so angry?"

"Nothing surprises me about how Paul behaves," Kara said, answering me, but her eyes and response were directed at Brad.

"That's enough, Kara," Brad said. The three of us stood there in silence for a few minutes. None of us had any idea what was the right thing to do.

"I'm cold. Let's go," Kara finally said as she motioned me to follow her to Brad's car.

"Should I leave him a note or something?" I asked no one in particular.

"He'll be fine," Brad said, opening up the back door for me, then holding open the door for Kara.

Brad let the car warm up; the hum of the engine was the only noise. When Brad drove to the front of the parking lot, he adjusted the rearview mirror so he could see my eyes, which were still a little damp. "Johanna, which way to your house?"

"Take a right," I said, slumping back in my seat as Brad accelerated.

"Okay, right it shall—"

Brad stopped in midsentence when he saw Paul's body crashing down on the hood of his car. I bolted up in my seat and screamed.

"What the hell?" Brad turned off the car, and we all jumped outside. Paul was lying on the ground next to Brad's car.

"Paul! Paul!" I knelt down beside him. I was so scared. "This is all my fault. Paul, are you okay? Oh, God, we need a doctor!"

Paul lifted his head off the pavement and motioned for me to come closer. "No doctor."

I could barely hear him.

"No doctor," Paul repeated. "I need, I need something else."

"What are you trying to say?"

"I need . . . I need a spoon," he said, pulling me closer with his left hand.

"A spoon?"

Paul started laughing. In his right hand he had a small bag, which he thrust at me. "Joha, I'm sorry. I just lose it sometimes. I promise it won't happen again."

I opened up the bag. Inside was a pint of chocolate-chip ice cream from Baskin-Robbins. In an instant the taste of my tears changed. The ones falling now were my favorite flavor and just as sweet as the ice cream.

THIRTEEN

"It is a good thing you didn't show up last night to Santi's," I whispered, which made little sense as Pam and I were about the only ones in the school library during first period. I had lied to Mr. Taylor about needing to do research for a story so the two of us could get out of class.

"What happened?" Pam asked.

I hit the highlights, leaving out the more unpleasant parts.

"So everything is okay between you now?" Pam asked.

"The evening had a very happy ending," I responded. I wanted to say more, to talk with Pam like we used to talk, but I felt myself holding back.

"Books, in these fantasy novels we read, there is a happy ending," Pam said, tapping her finger on the Tamora Pierce book in front of her. "I don't think real-life is like that."

"Maybe not," I said, but without much conviction.

"No offense, but I don't think Paul is exactly the prince type," Pam said.

"How come you never say anything nice about Paul?" I asked. Pam was trying to be funny and probably didn't mean anything by her comment, but it still hurt.

"How come you never say anything bad about him? I guess that evens things out," Pam shot back. "And besides, from what I hear, he's telling people all these lies about me."

"That's not the point." I stopped myself from raising my voice. The few other people in the library could have cared less about our conversation. No one was paying attention to us: Maybe that was the main thing that Pam and I once had in common. That had changed.

"The point is that you never call me anymore, and we never do anything together," Pam lashed out at me. We still saw each other every day in class and at our locker, but we never really talked. I could tell from Pam's tone that she was letting loose stored-up feelings.

"That's not true. I called you last Friday to see a movie," I countered.

"Sure, but you said we had to go to the early show so you could see Paul later that night. What is that?"

"Well, you never call me, either," I replied weakly.

"How could a person get through to you? If you're not out with Paul, then you're on the phone talking with him. I'm tired of hearing the phone ring, knowing you won't even interrupt your Paul call for a second to say hello to me. Call waiting? It's more like call ignoring."

I just wanted this to end. "Let's just drop this."

Pam leaned across the table. "Books, don't you want to be my friend anymore?"

"I do, but—"

"But what?" Pam spit out.

I didn't know what to say. I couldn't tell her the truth: that Paul was making me choose, and that I had chosen him over her. How do you tell a person something like that? I responded with silence.

"I miss spending time with my best friend. What is so wrong about that?" she asked.

She was right. Paul didn't want me to spend time with Pam or with anyone else but him. She was right, but I couldn't decide the other way. I couldn't lose Paul. "I do, too. I'm sorry Pam, but it just has to be this way."

I got up from the table and started to leave. She reached out and touched my left wrist. I let out a shriek of pain.

"Books, are you okay?" Pam asked. "What's wrong?"

"My wrist just hurts, that's all," I said as I tugged down on the sleeves of my blouse, making sure to cover the bruise on my wrist from Paul's punch.

"You see, this is what I am talking about?" Pam said, tears now flowing freely. "You don't share anything with me anymore."

"It's nothing," I said. Pam didn't need to know how Paul accidentally hurt me.

"But I'm not nothing. Don't you remember how I helped you when you first came to school here?" she continued through tears. "When Ty rejected you, I was there for you. Or have you forgotten that—like you've forgotten about me?"

"Pam, I haven't forgotten you; I just can't be friends like we used to be." It was so hard to confront someone like this; it took so much energy. "You can't have a friendship based on what was."

She turned to look at me; she never even blinked. "No, you can't, Johanna."

The sadness in my eyes was obvious. She quickly gathered her books, stood up, and walked out of the library just as the bell rang. Outside, I could see the hall fill up with students while I sat all alone in the school library. I had come full circle.

FOURTEEN

I was tapping the pencil against my calculus book, keeping time with Max Weinberg, the drummer for Springsteen's E Street Band. I had *Born in the USA* blaring in my Discman as I sat in the main library trying to force myself to work on the calculus problems lying in wait for me beneath the covers of the book. I ran my fingers up and down the sleeve of the black parka Paul had given me. He had opted for a leather jacket I picked out for him at the Goodwill he shops at. Looking at the book in front of me, I couldn't concentrate. I took the pencil and started drawing heavier lines around pictures of Paul and me that decorated the brown cover of *Calculus: Concepts and Problems*. I looked at my watch again, counting down the minutes until Paul would be picking me up. I sighed, looked out the window at the light snow falling, promising to make tomorrow's Thanksgiving a white one, and finally opened the book.

I had finished two problems during class, two more than anyone else had completed, so I just had one more to go. I wrote down the number *three* on a clean sheet of paper in front of me but found myself closing the book again, then writing the number *three* in big letters on the front cover. In just a couple of weeks, Paul and I would be celebrating our three-month anniversary. I never thought myself to be sentimental, but that number, more than all those equations glaring at me from inside the book, meant so much to me. I guess because I never thought it would ever happen. Now I was about to celebrate my best Thanksgiving ever. I opened up one of my notebooks and tore out a blank sheet of paper. I wrote at the top, "Things to be thankful for," and then Paul's name instantly. I sat there for a second, pulling Paul's parka around me tight, thinking about him holding me. I turned the Discman off, letting the sound of Paul's voice replace the Boss. I heard him whisper to me, "I want to touch you," and I remembered him saying that he loved me. I closed my eyes and just heard those words echo in my head, over and over again.

I took another sheet of paper out of my notebook. Yet another thing my father had drilled into me: work out your problems on paper, make your mistakes alone rather than in front of people. My dad wanted me to be like him, but now I was turning out so different. I'm sure he blamed Paul, never realizing that I was the one making the choices, and now even more choices were in front of me. I drew a line down the middle of the blank page, then wrote the words *yes* and *no* at the top. I stared at those words for a long time, my mind bouncing all over the place. I put my pencil in my mouth, shut my eyes, and tried to focus.

I stared at the paper, taking a quick look around to make sure nobody was watching me. This was so goofy, but it was how I did things. It worked for me. I crossed out the word *no* and made my list of questions on the side. It was the same list I went through when editing a story for the paper. I wrote down the words *who* and *why* and circled them; those I knew the answer to already. The words *where* and *when* came next, each followed by a big question mark. I shook my head thinking about the Firebird, knowing that would not answer the *where* question. I sat for a minute, gently rocking back and forth in the uncomfortable government-standard-issue library chair; then I wrote the word *how* with an even bigger question mark next to it.

I closed the notebook. This wasn't getting me anyplace. I didn't need questions; I needed answers. I waited until one of the library's computers was free, then barricaded myself in front of the screen, making sure that no one was watching over my shoulder as I typed. I pulled my red editing pen out of my pocket and wrote down the numbers of the books on the back of my hand. I went over to the shelf, watching to make sure no one was following me. I searched but was frustrated to find none of the books that were supposed to be on the shelf were there.

"Are you finding what you need?" a voice politely asked me.

I must have jumped an inch out of my new black high-top Converse All Stars. I turned around to see one of the librarians standing there. "Um, I was looking for some books."

"I see. Any particular subject?"

I walked over toward her, producing my hand like a suspect handing over evidence of a crime. "Um, these numbers."

The librarian smiled at me. I didn't know this woman's name, but she was always very helpful. She motioned me to follow her. I kept a step behind her, all the time looking around me. I wasn't doing anything wrong, but I felt so guilty. Like I was going to get caught, although I don't know at doing what. We stopped, and she handed me a book out of the young adult section. "Is this the type of book you are looking for?"

As soon as I glanced at the title *Changing Bodies, Changing Lives,* I wanted to crawl into a hole. I could feel myself blushing, but once again my body overpowered my will, and I stood there with my red cheeks flashing like a stoplight. I didn't say anything; I just took the book and hurried back to the table wishing I could have done so by going underground. I pushed all those important schoolbooks out of the way and opened this one up. I don't know where the time went as I read page after page, learning all the things that the "smartest girl in school" didn't know. I might know how to solve a quadratic equation, but I was obviously such an idiot. I knew this was the right book because everything was changing. I realized my question had changed from "should we?" to "when and where can we?"

"Excuse me." The librarian tapped on the edge of the desk. "Didn't you hear the announcement? We are closing now."

"What?" I quickly closed the page I was looking at, with the big heading "Birth Control" in letters that seemed ten feet high.

"We close at six tonight."

"Okay." I must have sounded like Lynne or Jackie: a total airhead, but I can get like that when I am reading something—totally engrossed in the words.

"Do you need to call for a ride?" the librarian asked me.

"No, I'm good." I started to gather up my textbooks that had spent the past two hours doing nothing but gathering dust. "I have a ride coming. He was supposed to be here at 5:30."

"Well, he's awfully late," she said.

"Not for him," I said. She laughed as she reached out and picked up the book from the table. "Thanks again for your help."

She just nodded, then smiled. "It was my pleasure."

I zipped up the parka and walked out in front of the library to wait, yet again, for Paul, who seemed to operate almost in his own time zone. They had just started to turn off all the lights in the library when I heard the sounds of the music pounding out the open window of the Firebird. Paul pulled almost onto the sidewalk, then pushed the passenger door open for me.

"I'm sorry I'm late," he said as I climbed in to find a Baskin-Robbins bag on the seat.

"It's okay, I was studying." I was hoping he wouldn't notice I was blushing. I didn't tell him what I had been learning about. I had decided soon, very soon, I would be showing him.

No sooner had I climbed in the car than Paul reached over to stick his index finger in the middle of my chocolate-chip ice cream. He laughed, then licked the ice cream off his fingers. When we reached the light at the ramp to the interstate, Paul dug his fingers deep into the ice cream, depositing a heap of it on my nose. As he was speeding up the ramp he leaned over and licked the ice cream off.

"Paul, that's enough." It was funny, but he was getting reckless.

He just looked at me, not saying a word. He took more ice cream and put it on my chin. He then reached across me to roll down the window.

"Are you gonna take care of this?" I asked, pointing at my face.

He looked over his glasses, his bright green eyes sparkling. "I thought I would wait until it dripped down a little lower before I licked it off." He then laid the brow on me, which he had mastered in no time.

"Well, if you don't let me close this window, I think it's going to freeze in place."

"Here it comes, listen!" Paul shouted as he dramatically turned the volume up on the CD. He threw his hand in the air, punching the inside of the roof of his car after each word, which he sang at the top of his lungs: *"It's a town full of losers, I'm pulling out of here to win"*!

"What are you doing?" I asked, shouting over the music turned up to the max.

"I'm celebrating that in about nine months I am so out of this death trap, this suicide rap."

"Can I roll the window up?" I asked.

"The Boss says, *'roll down the window and let the wind blow back your hair.'*"

"Well, I'm sure he didn't mean that to be true for a November Michigan night." I pulled a napkin out of the Baskin-Robbins bag and cleaned the ice cream from my chin.

"Don't question the Boss!" he shouted, slapping the back of his hand off my leg.

"What's so special about this song?" I asked, ignoring the bruise forming under my jeans.

"Did you know Bruce got the title 'Thunder Road' from a film of the same name, starring Robert Mitchum?" Paul was almost encyclopedic in his knowledge about stuff he cared for. I never understood why he didn't do better in school. I'd offered to help him with homework, but he'd always turn me down. Telling me, in words that never failed to get to me, that he wanted me for my body, not my brain. The few times we'd study together always ended up as a hands-on course in human anatomy.

"That line I was yelling, that's what matters. That's me giving the finger to Pontiac."

"I know it's not the best place in the world, Paul, but—"

"It's a suicide rap. You got to get out when you're young. I've survived here for seventeen years, so I'm pulling out of here to win." His words were racing almost as fast as the Bird was driving. "Only suits, like your folks, win this rigged game. It's the guys at the bottom that lose their jobs, lose their wives, lose their lives. I'm not going to be one of those losers!"

"Why are you so angry?" I asked, knowing I wouldn't get an answer. Paul gets like this sometimes, and you just can't reach him. The entire time he was ranting, he was slamming the steering wheel, like a doctor trying to start someone's heart.

"Brad and I got it all planned out. It's like running out of a burning building; there is no shame in it." He slapped my leg again, then pointed out the window at one of the closed auto plants we were driving past. "When I come back here from California, Pontiac won't even be here. There will just be a big For Sale sign stretching the length of the city."

I touched his arm gently, trying to calm him. "Paul, I wish you wouldn't talk this way."

"How else am I supposed to feel, Joha?"

I pulled his arm tight against me, trying to squeeze some of the anger out.

"You think I want to stay here? You think I want to be a trash bag all of my life? You think I want to live my father's life? You think—"

He stopped in mid-sentence. It was like a magic word for him: Whenever Paul would mention his father, he would shut down. It was like his heart pulled an off switch in his brain.

"No, I know you want more than that," I told him.

"Goddamn, Joha, don't you get it? I don't want more; I want it all!"

"You don't have to work in a factory," I countered weakly.

"This whole city is one big factory. Everyone just moves down the assembly line, surrounded by nothing but white noise and black shadows." Paul was getting wound up again. I tried to give his arm another squeeze, but he knocked my hands away. "More layoffs, it was in the paper today. The day before Thanksgiving. But do you know how many people in my class are hoping things will change? You take the honors classes, so you don't know people like this, but the school is loaded with them. They are hanging on to some dream of how life used to be here, believing the stories their parents and grandparents tell them about the glory days. You circle May 25 on your calendar. That is the day I graduate and leave all of this behind."

The breath went out of my body. I rolled the window up, then slumped against the side of the car. "Do you think on your way out of town that you'll have time to stop and say good-bye to me?"

He didn't even look at me. He ejected the *Born to Run* CD, and we sat there the rest of the way home in silence, the silence of white noise and black shadows.

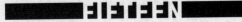

FIFTEEN

Dear Dead Dad:
The past few days have been crazy. I had a big fight
with Johanna the night before Thanksgiving. It was
one of those we just ignored the next time we saw
each other. For a smart girl she's pretty good at
playing dumb sometimes. She's good at rationalizing—
which is good, since I can be so irrational. Then I
had a huge blowup with Mom on Thanksgiving. I'm
still a little shook up by it all, but that is what
you're here for. You and the Stroh Brewing Company
can bring me down when I get too high and start me
up when I get too low. Sometimes I wish I could just
get stuck in neutral.

Before I met Johanna, Brad and me had made all
these plans, all these promises to each other and to
ourselves. I'm afraid of losing Johanna. I'm afraid
of losing all of my dreams because of her. She had
never been in the picture before, but now she is
smack in the middle and impossible to ignore. I know
everything we have shared has been true; those feelings are strong. But I know everything about my
plans to leave here are just as true and just as

strong. No wonder I sometimes drive in circles;
I am trapped in a round maze, my dreams chasing my
dreams. But sometimes I don't feel like a race-car
driver; instead, I'm more like the guy walking the
tightrope in the circus. Each day the tension in the
rope is increasing, the winds of change are blowing
harder, and my sense of balance is failing. Finally
Mom pushed me over the edge.

We were *celebrating* Thanksgiving. I don't really
know if that is the word you could use to describe
our sad little dinner. Mom spent all morning working
with folks from her church down at the homeless
shelter, so she didn't have time to make us much of
anything.

When Mom told me she wanted to talk, I knew it
was trouble. We had worked out a good arrangement
since you bolted. She prayed, and I stayed away. She
loved Jesus and preached her sermons, while I threw
fits and ranted. Quite the happy little household
you left behind. But then, you didn't really think
everything was going to be okay, did you? Who am I
kidding? You couldn't have cared less.

"What do you want to talk about?" I asked.

"We need to talk about college." I looked up at her, but was searching for a hole to suddenly open up in that crappy little trailer that I could disappear into.

"What about it?" I mumbled through my food.

"I know that you have your heart set on attending Stanford."

She wasn't looking at me; it wasn't a good sign. "I have told you many times that I would prefer that you attend Bethel or another Christian college."

I spit a piece of turkey onto my plate. "I don't think so."

"I know you don't want to attend those schools. This is a very hard decision for me."

"What is there to decide? I'm going to Stanford."

"Paul, there is just no money. When that man left, he left me with nothing but debts. That man just left, no note, no money, and no insurance when he finally died."

"Get over it! Dad's gone; get a new life." I threw my hands in the air. "This is bullshit!"

"You will not use that language in my house," she scolded me.

"Your house! Don't you mean your goddamned trailer!" I shouted back at her.

"How I pray for you, Paul."

"Don't waste your breath!" I stood up from the table.

"Please, Paul, sit down while we finish this meal."

I grabbed the tablecloth and pulled everything onto the floor. "There, it's finished!"

"You pick this up right now!" she shouted.

I just looked at her. "And if not? What are you going to do? What do you think you are going to do? You've already ruined my life!"

"I did not ruin your life. I love you, Paul." She bent down and started picking up the broken dishes. "There is just no money for you to go away to college."

I slammed my fist hard into the table, although I wanted it to be her face. "What am I going to tell Brad?"

"Paul, I love you. I am sorry. You should pray for guidance," she said.

"How do I face him? How do I face myself?" I knocked my chair onto the floor.

"You are just like that man," Mom said as she cleaned up the mess I left behind.

I ran right into my room and grabbed the phone. I punched in Brad's number so I could smash our plans. "Brad, listen—"

"Hello, bro," Brad answered. "Happy Thanksgiving!"

"Look, I got to tell you something," I was squeezing the phone so hard, I don't know how it didn't break in half.

"What's up, bro? Wedding bells? Shotgun shells?"

"No, it's something else. I'm serious." I was too angry to cry, too sad to scream.

"What's wrong?" Brad countered, realizing, for once, our conversation was not a laughing matter.

"I can't go to Stanford with you. I don't have the money. I let you down."

"Wait, we can figure something out I'm sure. A scholarship or—"

I didn't let him finish. "I don't want to talk about it. Look, don't tell this to anyone, especially Johanna, okay?"

"No problem," Brad replied.

"I'll tell her when the time is right, just not now. I can trust you, right?" I asked Brad, even though I knew the answer.

"Of course you can, Paul. I am always with you, right or wrong," Brad said.

"That's good, because everything is going wrong." I said it without an ounce of emotion in my voice; all my energy had drained from my throat to my hands forming fists. I slammed the phone down, but that wasn't good enough. I grabbed the phone and hurled it against the wall.

I turned my bed over and started running into the wall. Slamming over and over and over again, until my shoulder was bleeding. I heard Mom banging on the door, but I didn't care. I unlocked the door, almost knocking Mom over as I ran out to the Firebird. I gunned it, hitting the interstate in record time, the pedal pushing the floor and the car shaking like it was ready to explode. I kept pushing down the pedal, but there was only so far and so fast I could go. I drove until I saw that city-limit sign out on Telegraph Road. I rolled down the window; the snow-filled air chilled me down to my Chucks. When I passed the city-limit sign, I didn't cue up "Thunder Road" or scream out in defiance like before; instead, I hurled my *Born to Run* CD out the window and watched it smash against the pavement in this town for losers.

Did you do the same thing, Dad, the day you left town? Did you leave because your dreams didn't come true, either? Did you leave here because it became too much of a nightmare? I wish you would have taken me with you because I don't think I can do this on my own.

SIXTEEN

I twirled the key around my finger as I walked around my grand-parents' house. As I looked through the mail they had asked me to pick up while they were in Florida over the Christmas holi-days, I couldn't stop staring at the phone. I sat down at the kitchen table and took off my glasses, trying to think whom I could turn to for help.

Pam and I were acting like some old married couple. We ac-knowledged each other's presence, still shared the same locker, but our friendship was over. She was angry at me, and that was another thing we had in common: I was angry at me, too. It wasn't right to cut her out of my life like I did, but I knew that Paul didn't want me to share my time with anyone but him.

I thought about Kara. I didn't understand anything about Kara's life, but I thought she would understand what I was going through. She had probably gone through something like this a couple of years ago with Brad, but I knew I had nothing else in common with her. I remember Pam's put-down when she saw Kara and me standing together, saying to me: "Johanna, you are great books; Kara is great looks." I didn't think it was funny, mainly because I knew it was all too true. I liked hanging out with her and Brad; they were a lot of fun, even if sitting next to Kara made me feel like a troll. But even though I got to know

Kara a little during those nights out, she rarely talked to me at school. I realized she probably wasn't stupid, although sometimes I felt she and her friends played that part a little too well. But I knew that Kara was very good at getting what she wanted, which seemed to be either getting back in Brad's good graces or driving him crazy with jealousy.

Once I asked her what she was taking in high school, and she replied, "Mostly other people's makeup." She was a senior, but I never heard her talk about following Brad to Stanford, or even going to college. My guess is that Kara planned to hang around Pontiac with her best friends Jackie and Lynne, selling clothes at the mall and waiting for the next best thing. She was confident enough to know that she would always land on her feet.

I dumped my book bag contents on the kitchen table. I had her phone number in one of my notebooks, the result of some lame early attempt on my part to become her friend. With each ring I was half hoping that she wouldn't answer.

"Hello?" Kara said.

"Kara, hi, it's Johanna." There was a second of silence. Did she not know who I was?

"Wait a second; I've got Brad on the other line."

This was my chance. I could hang up, forget the whole thing. Pretend it never happened.

"I'm here."

"That was quick," I commented.

"Brad's like the Terminator. He'll be back."

I laughed. "How are you doing?" What a question. I could do better than that.

"Fine."

"Surprised to hear from me?" I sensed her discomfort, or at least slight confusion.

"Did you call to wish me a Merry Christmas?" Kara asked.

"Sure, but I didn't get you a present." Stupid. Could I say any more dumb things? I was going for a world record.

"That's cool, because I didn't get you one, either."

"Well, would you like to get me a present by doing me a really big favor? Can we talk?"

"We are talking." Kara was catching on to my cat-and-mouse games; I just didn't trust her enough yet. "Oh, you mean like talk, talk."

"Kara, this is hard." I wondered if she could hear me gnaw away a good portion of the thumbnail on my left hand.

"What's up?"

"You see, my grandparents are away in Florida, and I have a key to their house."

"So?"

"So, Paul wants to come over and—"

"So, what, you can't decide whether the two of you are going to finally—"

I took a deep breath. I obviously didn't have any secrets: My words went from Paul to Brad to Kara, but still I had to say it aloud. "No, I've decided what I am going to do. I mean, what we're going to do."

"Then I don't know what—"

"I need some excuse to get out of my house for the night. I want us to spend the night together. I guess that's silly."

"No, that's really sweet," Kara replied. "So you thought maybe I could—"

"Kara, I'm such an idiot. I'm sorry to have bothered you." I was trying to figure out how I was going to avoid seeing her the rest of the school year. This was just too embarrassing.

"No, wait up."

The line went dead for a second. I reached up and turned off the light in the kitchen. Conversations like this belonged in the dark.

"Okay, I got it!" Kara, normally so laid-back, sounded positively animated. "I pick you up like we're going to a movie. You call your parents from my house and tell them you're spending the night over at my house, some slumber-party bull. Then I drop you back at your grandparent's house and get you in the morning."

"What if they call for me at your house?" I quickly countered.

"Okay, wait a second." She sounded like she was pacing. "I'll give you my cell, and you just give them the number. They won't call, but just in case."

"How do you know they won't call?"

"Because they trust you. They don't even want to imagine something like this."

"Thanks, Kara." I was amazed. If she could solve tricky calculus problems like she solved my issue, she would have been first in her class. I had really misjudged her. "You know, I'm going to miss seeing so much of you once Brad goes to California."

"Well, maybe when Brad comes home. I guess you got lucky, now that Paul isn't going away to Stanford. The two of you can stay together all next year."

"What?" It was like 20,000 volts hit me. Paul wasn't going to Stanford? After that big scene before Thanksgiving and all that talk, he was staying?

"You mean Paul didn't tell you?" Kara asked.

"No!" My heart was racing: anger in one lane, happiness in the other.

"Looks like I screwed up. I'm sorry. I didn't know you didn't know," Kara said. She sounded mortified, but I wasn't mad at her.

"But he told you?"

"He told Brad that he didn't have the money to go away. Brad said he sounded pretty depressed about the whole thing. You know, that was all they talked about, moving to California together. Brad is torn up about it. He is so emotional, and he can't hide anything from me."

"Why didn't Paul tell me?" I was asking both her and myself the same question.

"Maybe he's embarrassed because he doesn't have the money. But this is good for you."

"Of course, I want him to stay here, but I know how bad he wants to leave."

"Everybody wants to leave Pontiac, everybody but me," Kara said.

"Kara, do you love Brad?" I had to take a chance to reach out to her and really connect.

"All my heart."

"Then how can you let him leave next year?" I asked, always thinking ahead.

For at least a minute I heard no sound but the furnace kicking on.

Finally she said, "I guess love isn't enough sometimes."

I mouthed the words, staring down at my notebooks covered with Paul's name. I was just a stupid girl with this naive crush; Kara was already a woman. Was I that innocent, or was she that ice-cold? I had to know. "But you could ask him to stay, couldn't you?"

"You're a smart girl, but if you think like that, you're going to get hurt, hurt real bad."

She had me pegged. For someone I had thought wasn't that

bright, Kara impressed me, while I was equally unimpressed with
my immaturity. I figured I might as well use it. "I guess I'm a little afraid about tonight, that's all."

"Is this going to be your first—"

"First time." I let out a deep breath, saying those words was
like lifting some weight.

"Well, you're already cooler about it than I was. I was, like, totally freaked. I heard these horror stories from friends and almost
chickened out. Just make sure Paul listens to you. You gotta let
him know stuff, you know what I mean?"

"Was Brad gentle for your first time?"

"He was cool, but he wasn't my first." Kara sounded indiffer-
ent to discussing the intimate details of her life.

"Oh."

"Don't be afraid or worried. You got some B.C.?"

"B.C.?"

"You know, birth control?"

"Paul is going to—"

"Good, don't end up like my friend Shana. She got a real
Christmas present last year, if you know what I mean."

"Kara, does it hurt?"

"It's like anything—you gotta do it for the first time, like
waterskiing I guess."

"I almost broke my leg the first time I went water-skiing." I
recalled the image of my prescription goggles flying in the air,
the skis flying over my head, and my butt smacking the water
with enough force to cause a tidal wave on the beach.

Kara laughed. "Well, like you'd *really* have to do it wrong for
that to happen."

"Can you do it wrong?" I didn't mean to say it aloud, but I
was glad I did.

"No, but it's not like some 'SinnyMax' movie. Just don't do anything you don't want to or that hurts too much. You have to draw some lines, I guess."

I couldn't believe it; I thought I had finally crossed all the lines, but Kara was telling me there were still more. I felt an urge to run back to the library and get that book in case I needed a reference at the ready. "How do you know?"

"You just do. God, listen to me talk," Kara sighed. "I sound like *Cosmo* magazine come to life. What you must think—"

"I think a lot of you for talking to me about this. You gave me some stuff to think about."

"Hey, I made the smart girl think! Maybe that was my Christmas present." Kara laughed, but I was mute.

She finally broke the silence. "Johanna, are you still there?"

"I'm here," I said.

"So, Johanna, is it on or off?"

SEVENTEEN

The house was mostly dark; I had set out only a few candles. Kara was right; my parents bought everything I was selling. When she dropped me off at my grandparents' house, she even gave me a little hug before I got out of the car.

I didn't realize that Paul had arrived. I had asked him to keep the music down, the windows rolled up, and to dim his lights when he pulled in the driveway. He lightly tapped on the door leading from the garage. I shut my eyes, trying to clear my mind, then let him in.

"Candles? Very nice," Paul said, walking in the door. "Looks like a church in here. Should I get down on my knees, or does that come later?"

"Maybe this way the neighbors won't notice," I said, quickly closing the door behind him. He took off his leather jacket and walked into the living room.

"I bought you something," Paul said, producing a Baskin-Robbins bag.

"Thank you." I took the bag and started for the kitchen.

"And I bought us something," he said, pulling a box of condoms from a brown bag. "These, by the way, do not go in the freezer."

I blushed, but quickly recovered with a raised eyebrow. "I assume you know where they do go?"

"If not, then I'll just have to practice until I get it right," he joked. "You look great."

I was wearing a new white sweater. Kara had talked me into going shopping before dropping me off. She was a maniac in the store, trying on outfits herself and suggesting ones for me. She was really pushing for this one dress: It was a long sleeveless blood-red gown. I had to talk my way out of not only buying it but even trying it on in front of her. That night at Santi's when Paul hurt my wrist wasn't the exception; it was becoming the rule. It seemed like he was always touching me: Sometimes a good touch, like tonight I hoped; but other times the touch wasn't soft. He would push me, grab my arms, jab his finger into me, or swat my arms and legs. It was a good thing it was winter; I could hide my black-and-blue skin under heavy sweaters. I just had to avoid clothes shopping with Kara, and I'd be okay.

"Want to look around?" I asked Paul.

"Up and down and all around," he said, forcing another laugh out of me.

I picked up one of the candles, and we walked down the hall-way. When we walked by my grandparents' bedroom on the first floor, Paul grabbed my hand and started in the room.

"Not here," I said softly. That would be just too weird. We walked up the stairs to a smaller bedroom on the second floor. I set the candle down on the small wooden table next to the bed, then took off my glasses, setting them on the table as well.

"Is the smoke from the candles bothering you?" Paul sat down on the bed. "It shouldn't. With your mom's habit, you probably secondhand smoke a pack a day."

I laughed, but then stepped away from him, walking over to the far wall. I touched the wallpaper. "When I was growing up, my parents were struggling a little. They worked lots of extra hours to get ahead, so I spent a lot of time here. I remember spending the night here so many times, but I was just a little girl then. It seems like a long time ago. And now—"

"Joha, come over here and climb in," Paul whispered as he pointed to the bed.

He was sitting on the edge of the bed; the candle behind him made him look like he was sparkling. I wished I was more like Paul. When he got angry, he screamed, and when he was happy, you could hear it in his voice. For me every emotion bore tears. All these years I have been waiting for someone like Paul to tell me it was okay to cry; tell me, like Paul always did, that "everything was going to okay;" and wipe my tears away.

I pulled my sweater off and set it carefully on the dresser. I didn't look at Paul during any of this; I looked at the floor, avoiding his eyes because I was embarrassed. I thought I heard him sigh.

"Joha, my back hurts. Would you rub it?" Paul took his sweatshirt off and tossed it on the floor.

I walked over toward the bed, bending down to blow out the candles.

"I would love to," I said, lying down on the bed next to him. "And I love you."

The morning was beautiful and clear, which disappointed me. I had hoped that during the night a terrible snowstorm would cover the city, trapping us in the house. We would be trapped where no one could reach us: not my parents, not Brad, not Kara, no one at all. Instead, the snow would cover the city, forcing us to huddle underneath the blankets to stay warm.

Last night, after the first time, Paul crawled out of bed and went into the kitchen. We sat up in bed eating chocolate-chip ice cream, laughing, and then made love again. I woke up once during the night, even though I didn't think I would ever get to sleep. My heart was beating so loudly, I thought the neighbors could have heard it. I woke up and was totally disoriented. I lay there listening to Paul's breathing, my heart beating in time. He would breathe in; I would breathe out. I lay staring at the ceiling, my eyes and mind both wide open. Was he satisfied? How long was it supposed to last? Why did this change everything between people? Why did it have to hurt like this?

I must have fallen back to sleep because I was startled awake by the alarm.

"What time is it?" Paul sat up in bed.

I put on my glasses and looked at the clock. "Almost nine. Kara's here in an hour."

I pulled the blankets up around me; I was freezing. "Can't we stay longer?" Paul asked.

Paul lay back down, pressing his naked body up against mine. He traced the outline of my body with his right hand. "Paul, we have to get ready to go."

Paul's arm came out from under the covers, reaching across me. He fumbled around on the table, plucking a condom from the box. "Come on, just once more."

"Really, Paul, no."

"Everything is going to be okay, trust me," Paul said in that reassuring tone that I had become so accustomed to and even so dependent upon. But I just couldn't.

"Paul, I'm a little sore."

"The doctor is in the house," Paul said, then tucked his head under the covers. "Let me try the classic prescription of kissing it and making it all better."

"Not now," I tried to push him away, but he grabbed my

arms and held them down. I finally managed to kick my legs out, pulling the covers with me. I landed on the floor with a thud.

"Come here!" He wasn't putting his arms out to welcome me like last night; instead, he was reaching down trying to grab me and pull me back into the bed.

"Paul, please," I said weakly.

Paul sat up in bed. "What's wrong?"

I crawled back over toward the bed, the blanket tight around me. I kissed his hand, which was dangling off the bed. "We'll have lots of time. Just not now, okay."

"When are your grandparents due back from this Florida trip?"

"Nine more days."

Paul bounced off the bed, landing on the floor next to me. He brushed up against me, then snuck his arm under the blanket. "That's good, because I want to do this again and again and again."

I poked him in the belly. "Casanova, I'm sure we'll work something out."

"Work!" Paul's head snapped back, like I had punched him in the gut.

"Is something wrong?" I asked.

"I have to work ten hours every day during break. When I'm not at work, I gotta do a stupid *Moby Dick* paper for English class. You wanna write it for me?"

I laughed; I didn't think he was serious. "How much you gonna pay me?"

He flicked his fingers across my lips. "I don't know; maybe we could work out a barter system. You do for me, and I do for you."

"We'll see about that."

"Hey, let's take a shower," Paul said as he tried to pull the covers off of me.

"Okay, but turn around first, please," I requested.

"What?"

"Turn around while I go into the bathroom," I said softly.

"So now you're the funny one. Some joke," Paul said with a laugh.

"Please."

"I don't think so. Do you know how long I've wanted to see you like this?"

"Paul, I'm serious," I said, trying to avoid looking him in the eye.

"Well, you need to yuk it up then." Paul shrugged his shoulders, then ripped the blankets off of me. He dove on top of me and started tickling me. He was laughing; I wasn't.

I pushed his hands away. "Stop it."

"Fine, just forget it," he said as he jabbed his finger hard into my shoulder. I ran into the bathroom, picking up his sweatshirt on the way.

No sooner had I caught my breath than Paul pounded on the door. "Come on out here!"

As I started to open the door I heard a loud noise that sounded like Paul giving a piece of my grandparents' furniture a stiff kick.

"I'm sorry," I started. "I'm sorry if I upset you."

Paul put on his jeans and sat on the bed. "We don't have much time, that's all. It's not like I'm going to be here forever."

"What do you mean?" I asked as I stepped out of the bathroom and next to the bed.

"I'll be leaving for Stanford soon. It's not that far away," Paul said.

I started to correct him. I had been waiting for him to bring the subject up ever since my conversation with Kara. The timing of this was giving me an uneasy feeling in my stomach.

"Joha, sometimes I wish I wasn't going away." He pulled me down on the bed next to him. "I hate to go because I feel so close to you, especially after last night."

I felt like I was being prompted to say something, something like "please don't go," but the words would not come.

He reached over to the table. He picked up his glasses and put them on. He hugged me. Then he took his class ring and put it on the ring finger of my left hand. "I think last night changed things, don't you?"

I buried my face in his shoulder, hoping those words were true. Hoping that now, every touch from Paul would be soft and loving. "Paul, I would miss you if you went away, but I know that is what you want. If you stayed here, you would hate it and eventually hate me."

"I could never hate you," he said, pulling me tight against him. "Besides, it's only for one year, then you could join me at Stanford."

I pulled away from Paul; this was way too much for me. I had spent a lot of time hearing about Paul and Brad's California plans, but we never talked about mine. My parents were convinced I was headed to the University of Michigan to become an engineer, just like my dad; but those weren't my dreams. I was set on the school of journalism at Columbia in New York. I had yet to tell Paul or my parents about my dreams.

"Think about it, you and me, Brad and Kara, all living out California way."

"I don't think Kara is going to California with Brad."

"I think that's a big mistake. A big mistake. They should be together."

I just nodded my head; I didn't have the energy to speak anymore.

Paul wrapped his arms around me, pulling me toward him. "I think they should be together . . . we should be together. I don't think I could live a year without you. I don't see how I've lived almost eighteen years without you. You're the most important thing in my life. This is my late Christmas present to you. I won't go to Stanford. I will stay here for you."

I closed my eyes, pretending like I was asleep and this was all just a dream. Because I had dreamed it, but dared not speak it. I had dreamed this speech from Paul, dreamed him saying that I was the most important thing in his life. I dreaded the day he would leave. The past months had been the best of my life. I loved him more than ever, but I knew. Again he said all the right things, but for all the wrong reasons.

"Joha, what's wrong? Why the tears?" He reached down and gently touched my face again, wiping away my tears. He licked the end of his fingers. "If your grandmother were here, what flavor would she say these are?"

I tasted these tears, bitter tears of sadness running down my face.

I never even looked up. "Tears of joy," I said.

EIGHTEEN

"Do you want to explain this?" My mother asked as she barged into my room.

I was on the computer, responding to an E-mail from Paul about plans for the Valentine's Day dance, which was under a month away. I knew he hated dances, and anything "formal and normal," as he called it, but this was special to me. Two and a half years, and I'd never been to a school function like this. I wanted to see how the other half lived.

"Are you listening to me?" My mother's voice raised on each word, no doubt made louder by the silence of my response. "I asked you, young lady, have you seen this?"

She brandished my third-quarter report card like it was a rock she was going to bash over my head. I knew this was coming. I can't say that I blamed her for being upset with me. She wasn't the only one concerned. My teachers, in particular Mr. Taylor, were worried about my falling grades. I knew there was no way I could make them understand that pleasing Paul was more important to me than passing every class with straight A's.

"Paul! Paul! Paul! Is that all you can think about anymore?" I could tell she was furious. Normally, when she was raving like this, she left a trail of smoke behind her, like a jet engine; but she must have run up to my room between cigarettes.

"Are you going to say anything?" Her impatience was evident, if not unexpected.

My new approach to her query bombardment was to wait until the final question. That way, I could maybe get away with ducking a few of the questions I knew she wouldn't like the answer to, or questions that I just couldn't give a response to, for both our sakes.

"I am talking to you, young lady." She was shouting at me, but I was letting the words bounce off of me without leaving a mark. I guess Dad was toughening me up after all.

"What has happened to you, Johanna Marie?" My mother followed me as I got up from the desk and headed over to my bed. There was no place for me to run. I was trapped, but she was the one acting like the caged animal.

"Please, just leave me alone." I said it through tears, the words grinding out through those teeth my parents paid to have straightened. That is when they were happiest: when they were straightening me out.

"No, I will not leave you alone, not until I get some answers." Her voice was down one decibel, now only audible within a one-square-mile radius. She tossed the report card down in front of me. "Are you ready to explain this to me?"

"Mom, I know. I need to do better." I almost laughed as I thought of all the happy households where my classmates were bringing home report cards worse than mine and getting hugs. It was that my report card didn't have the A's stacked like firewood. There were only two of them; but they were surrounded by two ugly B's that buzzed in the middle and a C in physics sticking out like a broken thumb.

"Do you know what your father is going to say when he sees this?" I had an idea.

"I know." I was lying on the bed, face-down because I couldn't face any of this.

"You know why your grades are suffering, don't you?"

I didn't answer. I knew the answer; so did she. And I knew she would tell me.

"You're spending too much time with Paul. We thought we could trust you to show good judgment, to manage your time." Time management was yet another thing my father drilled me on. He had made me read *The Seven Habits of Highly Effective Teens.* He told me to avoid what he called "time bandits," which are people who wasted your time. In his mind Paul should be indicted for grand theft. My mother raved on. "It looks like we were wrong, doesn't it?"

I was burying my face in my pillow; I couldn't answer any of these questions. They were right, but they were also wrong. So very very wrong.

"If you're not spending time with him, then you are talking with him on the phone. Do you know how much time he is stealing from you?"

That wasn't fair. "He isn't stealing anything."

"You're right; you're giving it away. You should be studying now, but there you are on the computer writing him."

"What am I doing so wrong?" I sat up in bed and clutched the pillow in front of me. A question like this was as close to a confrontation as I got with my mother.

She laughed. "You don't study. You don't wear the nice clothes I buy for you; instead, you look like a walking Goodwill ad. You've made too many changes too fast that we are not happy with."

I took a deep breath, then inched closer to the edge of the

bed. I made sure I looked at the floor, avoiding direct eye contact. That would be suicide. "Well, I like them, and so does Paul."

"It doesn't matter what he thinks. He doesn't own you, does he?"

I wanted to jump up and shout, "Neither do you," but I couldn't go that far. Instead, I said nothing.

"You wear his clothes. That's his parka there on the door. Those sweatshirts are all his. You wear his class ring. You listen to his music. What is happening to you?"

"I can handle it." I still couldn't look at her when I spoke.

She came back to the bed, standing over me. I could see the tension eating away at the corners of her eyes and mouth. "You only have time for him, and nothing else."

I was exhausted. My mother's constant questions wore me down.

I got up off the bed and reached for Paul's parka hanging on the closet door. I had to escape. I had to see Paul. I needed his reassurance that I could get through this. I needed to hear him say "Everything is going to be okay." I started toward the door. "Can I go now?"

"We are not done here." My mother grabbed my desk chair and pushed it right in my path toward the door. "Sit."

As I eased into the chair I had a bad muscle memory. This was one of my father's favorite punishments when I was a child, making me sit still in a chair when I did something wrong. He would demand I sit quietly sometimes for up to an hour. If I started to cry, he would say nothing; but the look, the look was so hard and so cold. I think that's when I learned to shut down, and I vowed never to cry in his presence, or in public.

"You will spend more time on your studying, agreed?" She pointed at the report card.

"I know, I know." I shook my head, half in anger at her, half in disgust at myself for falling short of my goals and for failing to have perfect grades.

My mother grabbed the report card off the bed, dropping it on my lap. "Good, I am glad we agree. You'll start by spending less time with Paul, beginning tonight."

I knew this was coming. They had grounded me, discouraged me, but this was the first outright ban. This was my moment of truth.

"No."

"What?"

"I said no." I didn't move a muscle. I didn't shed a tear. I was almost calm, even if inside I was shaking like an earthquake had struck my heart.

"What did you say?" She was pretending to be hard of hearing, but she wasn't blind to the fact I was standing up to her—even if I did so by remaining perfectly seated and positively calm.

She paused. I think she was so used to my giving in, she really didn't know what to do. She walked away from me and sat on the edge of my desk. She sat there for the longest time, shaking her head in disgust.

"Johanna, you shouldn't spend so much time with one person at your age," my mother said, her tone shed of the heat of hostility, replaced now with the warmth of motherly wisdom; but I wasn't fooled. "Your father and I want you to be happy. You need to spend time with other people."

"I don't want to see anyone else."

"What about your friends?"

"Mom, I don't want any other friends." I wanted to remind her that I didn't really have any other friends. I wanted to say, "Mom, I can't do everything," but that ran counter to what my parents and even some of my teachers, believed.

"How about Pam? She used to call and come over all the time. What happened with her?"

"Pam and I had a falling out," I said, sadness and shame creeping up my throat. "Anyway, I just want to spend my time with Paul; that's all that I want."

My mother moved from the desk toward me. She reached out and touched the side of my face. "Johanna, you're still very young. You think you're grown-up just because you can do grown-up things like kiss, but you are only sixteen. You'll have lots of time later to worry about boys after high school or college. That can wait. What you need to focus on now is things like getting good grades in school, right?"

"What I need is Paul," I repeated, thinking about how happy he made me, thinking how my mother wanted to take away the only thing that really made me happy. The good grades, the award-winning projects, my parents shared those things with me; Paul was all mine.

She stood up, the gentleness vanished from her voice when she realized the new and nice tactic wasn't working either. "I'm talking about important things."

Those words were more painful than anything she could have done to me physically. "And Paul isn't important?"

My mother took a few steps behind me. She must have known how deep her words had cut me. She was trying to sneak away from the chalk outline she had left of me on the floor. "No, he cannot be as important as your grades. You have to learn to put things in perspective. One day you'll see that I am right."

"That's not fair."

She walked past me, leaving me sitting there in the chair. "We're done discussing this. I will not tell you that you cannot see Paul. We trust that you will come to that conclusion for yourself. But you will see less of him. That is what is best for you."

My fingers clawed at the chair. "That is what is best for you, not for me."

She put her hand on the doorknob. "One night a week, that is all. Starting now."

I started to cry; she had won. She had won again, damn her. "That's not fair."

I was turning the chair to sawdust with my fingers; I was grinding my teeth to the root. I was doing everything I could do to not scream in total defiance.

"You have to trust us on this. We love you, Johanna, and want only what is best for you."

"You tell me to trust you; then you hurt me like this," I said, tears welling in my eyes. "You say you love me, but you hurt me."

My mother never turned around. She opened the door; she never bothered to close it. I guess she wanted my dad to know that she had reduced me to a crying little girl.

NINETEEN

Paul slowly turned the car into the school parking lot. We were late, of course, so there was no parking up close, and worse, someone had the nerve to take Paul's special spot.

"I'll park behind the cafeteria, although I'm afraid the smell will rot the paint off the Bird," Paul joked.

"But that's so far to walk in this cold." The temperature was around zero with the windchill around minus ten.

"I'll keep you warm," Paul said, giving my knee a squeeze, then reaching into a large paper bag he had brought with him. "And I'll keep you cool."

He showed me the pint of chocolate-chip ice cream, which would not be melting in this frigid weather. I smiled and kissed him on the cheek.

"I'll keep my engine running," Paul said as he pulled the car into the almost deserted parking area. "And maybe I'll get your engine started."

I rolled my eyes; it was becoming my most common reaction to Paul's fondness for sexually suggestive double entendres.

Paul placed a small package, wrapped with shiny red paper on my lap. "I decided to burn a CD for you as a Valentine's Day gift. So when we're apart, you'll have our songs."

My gift to him, a new Springsteen biography, seemed so lame

compared to this. I vowed to myself to do better next year; but I had just been so busy with getting my grades up that as much as I thought about Paul, I just never got my mind around a gift, and I didn't want to ask my parents for the money. Besides, he always seemed happier giving gifts than getting them.

I reached for the ice cream. "Open the gift first," Paul directed me.

I was very careful about taking off the paper; I could sense that Paul was getting impatient with how long it was taking me. He probably had never noticed, but I was keeping everything. Every time he gave me a gift, I kept not just the gift, but the box, the wrapper, the bow, the card, anything and everything. This archive had been a great source of comfort to me for the past few weeks since the once-a-week rule had gone into effect. I think my parents were surprised that I picked Wednesday nights rather than the weekend. What they didn't know was that while Paul's mother was attending church, we were doing our impersonations of Adam and Eve in his bedroom. Or as Paul liked to call us having sex: "visiting the grandparents."

"I want you to think about me when you listen to these," he said.

While I looked at the list of songs Paul had typed up on the cover, he pushed in the disc. As the first song, "If I Should Fall Behind," played, we started steaming up the windows.

I was lost in his touch, the pressing of our bodies against each other and the texture of his lips. Paul and I were spending as much time together as we could. If my parents' goal was to pull us apart, it had backfired. Our time together grew even more intense. I was beginning to feel it was Paul and me against the world, with my parents representing the world. They were wrong about Paul, and I was going to show them.

I found myself drawn closer to Paul, even though he lied to me about Stanford. It didn't matter why Paul was staying, and I could understand why he didn't tell me the real reason. The important thing was that he wasn't going anywhere, and I couldn't be happier.

"C'mon, let's go in," I said. As much as I was enjoying Paul's touch, I wanted to get inside.

Paul pushed the CD out of the player, stuck it back in the cover, and then dropped it into his pocket. We locked up the car, then locked arms walking toward the gym.

"I'm going to get him to play one of your songs." No sooner had Paul and I dropped off our coats than he raced off toward the DJ. I knew that Paul was going to try to charm him into playing the songs on my CD and get the Boss shaking the rafters.

I smiled and gave him a mock salute, as if wishing him luck on some important mission. These things mattered to Paul; he could be so passionate about his music, it was useless to try to talk him out of it. Better just to let Paul be Paul than to try and change him.

I looked up toward the front of the gym. Paul had the DJ laughing, which was a good sign. I just shook my head and started looking for somewhere to sit. Pam was there with Dylan Baxter, a geeky nice-guy who was in honor's physics with us. Kara and Brad hadn't arrived yet. I saw Mr. Taylor talking with a few students near the door, but I was doing my best to avoid him. I didn't want to talk with him, mainly because I was afraid of what I might tell him. What was going on between Paul and me didn't need to be shared with anyone, for any reason.

"Johanna, over here!" The voice came from one of the back tables.

I turned around. There was Marcus, a new student who transferred in last month. He was a great photographer, and we were lucky to have him join the newspaper. I had gone out of my way to talk to him, remembering how alone I felt my first few months being the new kid in school.

"Hi, Marcus." I walked over to him. He was sitting with only his camera for company.

"Smile." He dropped down to one knee, flashing my picture over and over.

"Hey, that film is expensive!" I joked, grabbing a seat next to him.

"Don't worry, Chief, it doesn't belong to the paper," he responded. He had adopted Brad's nickname for me by his second day in class. "I'm taking pictures for the junior class. Only five dollars. That's a two hundred percent markup, but it's for a good cause. 'Cause us juniors need the money."

Marcus had a great sense of humor, an engaging smile, and was doing 200 percent better at making friends than I did my first year.

"If I can ever get Paul to come sit with me, maybe I'll take you up on that," I said.

"That's cool. So, what's he doing?" Marcus said pointing at Paul, who high-fived the DJ and was headed back toward the table. "Does he have a part-time job as a DJ?"

"No, he's just being Paul. That's a full-time job." I stood up and started waving toward Paul. He worked the crowd a little while Marcus and I small-talked.

"So, what's with the new boyfriend?" Paul said, when he arrived at the table.

I just shook my head. "This is Marcus; he works for the paper. I've told you about him."

Paul slapped him on the arm, then pointed to his camera. "Nice, but not a digital, huh?"

"No, old school."

"Should have gone with the digital, Marcus," Paul said, slipping behind me and putting his hands over my shoulders. "No one has to see them, so you never know what might develop."

"I'll remember that," Marcus said, rising from the table.

I laughed and waved good-bye. Paul didn't acknowledge Marcus as he left the table.

"Success?" I asked, pointing to the DJ.

"I think so," Paul said as he sat down next to me. "So, is he the backup boyfriend?"

"What?"

Paul leaned against me, putting his hands over the top of mine, squeezing them tight. "Since you only see me one night a week, maybe you got somebody for the other six nights."

"Paul, that's silly." I was laughing, but he didn't crack a smile.

"Whatever." Paul slumped back in his seat. "When is this crap going to end?"

"Paul, it's not my fault."

"You should just tell your parents off."

I leaned over toward him. "I can't do that."

"I tell my mom that all the time. When are you going to stand up to them?"

"I can't talk to them like that."

"Can't or won't? Maybe if you went out with Marcus of Kodak that would be okay?"

"Paul, let's talk about this later. Can't we just have a good time?" I begged.

"A good time, as long as it is once a week, right?" He bounced his fist off the table.

"You just don't understand what my parents are like." I was talking slowly, logically, and calmly. I had to make him see my point of view. "You don't know what it's like to have parents like mine. My father—"

As soon as the words left my mouth, I knew I had made a terrible mistake. He pushed the table away, then started toward the door. Not even the sound of "If I Should Fall Behind" filling the room stopped him. He grabbed his coat from the rack and raced outside.

The freezing wind chilled my face once I grabbed my coat and left the school building. I couldn't just see my breath, I could hack it with an ice pick. The arctic wind just bounced my own words back to me. "Paul! Paul! Where are you?"

I made it to the car, but while the Bird was there, Paul was nowhere to be seen. I didn't know what to do. I didn't want to ask anyone else for a ride; that would just make him even more jealous. I couldn't leave him out here. This was all my fault. I knew better than to mention Paul's father. I never asked; he never told.

In the distance, I thought I heard Paul crying. I had actually never seen or heard him cry, so I was guessing.

"Paul? Is that you?" No answer.

"Paul, please answer me. I'm scared." The quiver in my voice sounded like a warped recording. No answer.

"Paul!" I was screaming now, pulling punishing gulps of frozen air into my lungs. The source was close now. I navigated the snow piles the best that I could with heels, tracking the fresh footprints in front of me thanks to my years as a Girl Scout.

The sound was louder, the wind was colder, and my lungs were ready to explode.

There he was.

Paul was kicking the huge green Dumpster behind the cafeteria. He was kicking it with the force of a fireman breaking down the door of a burning house. Over and over and over, he slammed his foot against the metal.

"Paul, stop that!" I shouted as I tried to run over to him.

He gave the container one last stiff kick, and then turned to face me. It was dark, so there were no details to take in. He was dressed almost all in black; there was no smile shining toward me. There was no moonlight to bounce off his green eyes.

"Leave me alone." He was breathing heavily.

"Paul, I'm freezing," I said, reaching a hand out toward him. "Let's get in the car."

He put his head down and walked right past me.

I followed close behind him, which was easier than I imagined. Even though I was skating on ice with heels, he was limping. I had to imagine, from what I had heard and seen, that his foot, or at least a couple of toes, must be broken.

I was standing by the passenger-side door. The light was better, but I saw no tears in his eyes. I didn't say anything; all my well-crafted words had no use here.

"Paul, let's go, please." I tried to wrap my arms around him, but he pushed me away.

"Leave me alone."

"Paul, please, it's freezing—"

"I said leave me alone, or are you as deaf as you are dumb?"

He looked so lost, so damaged. I just wanted to hold him. "Everything is going to be okay." I said the words softly, just as he had said them to me so many times when I was worried, upset, or scared.

The look he gave me was one that I had never seen. Worse than the looks my father gave me. If looks could kill, I would be dead.

"What did you say?" No cold air went into his lungs as his teeth were clinched too tight.

"I said everything is going to be okay."

"Listen, don't you ever say that to me again." He jammed his index finger hard into my collarbone. His breathing was heavy; his tone, icier than the wind blowing over both of us.

"But Paul, I just meant—"

"This is all your damn fault, Johanna." His face was two inches from mine, but it could have been two hundred feet, and I could have heard him as loud as his voice was now.

I was crushed between him and the car. I couldn't move. "Please, I'm freezing."

"Poor you. You are cold; isn't that too fucking bad. Yours is such a hard life!" Paul screamed at me. He took one step back, then pushed me hard up against the car with all of his strength. I seemed almost to bounce off the car back toward him. I was too stunned to do, to say, even to feel, anything. I could feel the tears freezing as they rolled down my face.

"Get your fat ass in the car!" Paul said as he opened up his door, but I couldn't move. I was paralyzed: The blood was rushing to my face and out of my heart.

Paul turned the music up loud, then pushed the passenger door open. I let instinct win over intellect and climbed in.

We drove around—without a word between us—for almost an hour, before Paul pulled into a 7-Eleven. He kept the car running, and that was all I could think of as well: running away. But the physical pain and my utter confusion kept me stuck in my seat. I sat back and started gnawing on my nails.

Paul returned a few moments later with a grin on his face and a six-pack of Stroh's in his hands.

"You want one?" he asked as he got back in the car.

"No," I said very firmly.

"Whatever," he said, peeling out of the parking lot. We drove around the back streets of Pontiac listening to Springsteen while I held back tears and Paul downed beers, tossing the empty cans into the backseat. There was nothing to say. As Paul finally pulled off the freeway and headed toward my house, he turned down the music and leaned against me.

"Look, Joha, I'm sorry," Paul said.

"Please, Paul—"

"I want you to kiss me," he said, pulling me closer to him. Before I had a chance to answer or act, Paul jerked the car to the side of the road. We were about a mile from my house on a stretch of road without any houses. Paul turned off the lights.

"I said, I want you to kiss me," he repeated softly into my ear, although the words were slightly slurred. "I bet if I were Marcus, you would want to kiss me."

I tossed my hands in the air. "Paul, that is so wrong. Why are you playing these games?"

"You want to play games, Johanna. We'll play games," he said, crawling into my seat, lying on top of me.

"Paul, get off me." I tried to push him off, but he was too strong.

"How about this game?" He was totally on top of me, his hands pinning down my arms. His weight made me unable to move, or even breathe.

"Please, Paul."

Paul thrust his arms underneath my coat and my sweater. "What's wrong with this game?" His elbow was digging into my stomach as he roughly squeezed my breasts.

"Get off me, please." I tried to get away, but he was pressing down too hard against me.

"What's wrong? Marcus wear you out?" Paul's eyes were dead.

"Paul—" But that name really meant nothing. I didn't know this person looking at me with such anger. I didn't want to know this person. I just wanted to get away.

"Shut up! Where is Marcus now? Why don't you call him to come save you? Is Marcus who you are going to be with when you abandon me? Is he?" Paul screamed at me.

"Paul, stop!" He pulled his hands from under my sweater and tried to cover my mouth.

"Shut up! Isn't there something better you could do with your mouth than run it?" I heard him shout as he unzipped his pants.

"Don't touch me!" I screamed, still trying to push him off me.

"Oh, I'm done touching," he said, smashing the back of his hand hard across my face. The second blow was with the palm. It was with more force. It drew blood from my nose and sent my glasses flying. The third was another backhand shot, so hard I think it loosened some of the teeth my parents had paid to have straightened. He moved off me and collapsed in his seat.

I reached out with my right hand and pushed the car door open and fell out onto the pavement. I scrambled to get to my feet. I started running; although with no moon in the sky and no glasses on my face, I was almost blind. The tears running down my face and the blood flowing from my nose made it hard to breathe, but still I ran.

I had made it only a few yards up the road when the Firebird roared up behind me. I heard the door slam, and seconds later Paul was pulling me toward him.

"I'm sorry, Joha, I'm so sorry." He grabbed on to me, smothering me in his arms. I was exhausted. I couldn't fight him and win. He picked me up, an inch off the ground, and pulled me back to the car. I tried to push away, but I didn't have the strength; his grip was too tight.

"Joha, let me explain," Paul said, pushing me into the car. I thought about making a run for it, but even if I got away, this scene would just be replayed over and over again.

He reached out to wipe the tears from my eyes, but I turned away, crunching myself into a little ball in the corner, the safest shelter I could find.

"Joha, I didn't mean it. I'm so sorry. I just—" He handed me my glasses.

"Take me home." I don't know how he could understand anything I was saying. I was speaking through the noise of the tears, sniffles, and heavy breathing.

"Let me explain."

"I don't want an explanation." I was hissing the words. He didn't say anything. He turned the music off, so the only sound was my out-of-control crying.

Before the car came to a complete stop in my driveway, I opened the door. I tried to escape, but he grabbed on to my left arm and tried to pull me back inside.

"Joha, let me make it up to you—"

I looked down at his hand touching mine, then looked him right in those green eyes.

"Joha, I don't know what else you want me to say. I said I was sorry. Let's just forget it. Everything is going to be okay, trust me."

"No, everything is not going to be okay!" I shouted. I jerked my arm away from him and slammed the car door behind me. My eyes filled with tears. I knew the taste of these tears, although they were new to me. These were tears that tasted of never again. It was over.

TWENTY

My mother was at the front door, but she never got a word out of her mouth. I raced through her smoke screen, going past her so fast that she didn't get to ask one question about, or take a close look at, the blood trickling down my nose or the tears running down my face. I hit the stairs in a dead run, taking them two at a time. I flung open the door to my room and tossed Paul's parka onto the floor, then locked the door behind me.

I grabbed a T-shirt—a Springsteen T-shirt that Paul had given me—from a drawer and used it to wipe away the blood from my nose. I hurled the T-shirt onto the floor, tossing it away from me like it was garbage. I wanted to cry, but I heard my mother's footsteps coming up the stairs.

"Johanna, what's wrong?" she said, knocking on the door.

I couldn't speak. I couldn't tell anyone, especially her. I wanted to be Alice and disappear down the rabbit hole.

"I want you to open this door, do you hear me?" The pounding grew louder.

I took a deep breath and walked toward the door. I leaned against it but didn't turn the knob.

I looked down through my tears and saw the doorknob twisting. "Johanna Marie, you open this door right now!"

I unlocked the door and quickly turned away, my mind racing

to invent the lie that would keep me free from both her questions and her contempt.

"You know you are not supposed to—" my mother started, but stopped when I turned around for her to see my face.

"What is going on here?" she asked, but the tone was not that of the Grand Inquisitor but one of real concern for my well-being.

"I fell on the ice in the parking lot at school. I'm okay, just a little bruised." I tried to hide my eyes from her the entire time I spoke.

I waited, praying that she would believe me. To speak the truth, to tell her that Paul did this, to admit that she was right and I was wrong—that I couldn't do. Not now, not yet. Not ever.

"Do you need me to take you to the hospital?" my mother asked, her instincts for control overcome by her primal instincts of motherly love for an injured child. "What can I do?"

I paused again, considering the question. I needed someone to talk to about this, but it couldn't be her. "No, it's not that bad. I just need to sleep, that's all."

"Let me get you some aspirin and a cold compress," my mother continued, not willing to let go.

"I'm fine, really, Mom," I said, very softly, almost in a whisper.

"That doesn't look fine to me," my mother said as she started out of the room. "I'll be right back."

There was no use in disagreeing with my mother; I would never win. As she walked away, determined to do what she wanted rather than what I said I needed, it became so clear to me. I had been able to hide the bruises from her under clothes, but this one I couldn't cover. Nor did I think I would be able to hide my hurt from breaking up with Paul. The solution was so simple. When my mother pushed, I wouldn't push back. I wouldn't argue or disagree. If I went along, I could get along. With no fighting, there would be no questioning. If there was no questioning, then my shame from this night would remain secret.

My mother returned, setting two aspirins and a glass of water on my desk, then handed me the cold compress. To my surprise, she then hugged me and kissed me gently on the forehead. "Johanna, if you need anything . . ."

"I know Mom, I know," I said, but that was the whole problem. I wanted to give in to my need for her, but as long as I needed her, she could control me. My life wouldn't be my own; it would be hers. No. This was the night my life would start. I was taking it back from my mother, back from Paul. This throbbing pain in my face felt like the new me laboring to be born.

"I love you, Johanna," she said, then hugged me again and walked away. I collapsed next to the door, listening to her footsteps, then the sound of her bedroom door closing. I rubbed my hand against my face, feeling the damage done. How could those hands that had touched me so gently, that had moved me with passion, have done this to me?

I stared up at the ceiling. I felt like it was pushing down on my chest, but it was just the memory of Paul on top of me. No wonder I couldn't take a decent breath. Reaching up to touch the side of my face again, I could feel the bruise forming. How was I going to explain this away? I had been able to hide the bruises on my arms from when Paul hurt me before, but how could I explain this to anyone? I rubbed my hands over it again and again, trying to make it go away, trying to erase it from my face and the memory of it from my mind. I moved my hands up a little and felt the star-shaped earrings dangling from my lobes.

I jerked the earrings off. Like a woman possessed, I crawled over to my desk. I pulled the bottom drawer out, tipping the contents on the floor: the wrapping paper, the boxes, the cards, the ribbons, and the bows. I emptied the trash can next to my desk, then dumped into it all those precious souvenirs. Beneath them were ticket stubs to movies and all the Baskin-Robbins bags. I went over to my books and pulled out the ones that had the rose petals pressed in them. The rose petals were silent as they floated into the trash.

I opened the door and looked, to make sure my parents' bedroom door was closed. I picked up the trash can and lugged it downstairs into my father's office. On a low shelf I found a bunch of big mailing envelopes and dumped the mass of paper into them. In my right hand I clutched the earrings. I hesitated for a second, and then tossed them inside. I grabbed a sheet of paper and a pen, getting as far as "Dear Paul" until I realized, words meant nothing and tossed the paper into the trash.

I wrote Paul's name and address in big bold letters on the envelopes, then sealed up all the evidence of our past together. I covered the envelopes with stamps, but didn't put a return address on them. From the hall closet I grabbed my old long coat, and then found my mother's car keys on the kitchen table.

I drove a couple of miles to the nearest post office. I kept the car running and took the envelopes with me. Balancing the envelopes on the top of the mailbox, I opened the door, but I couldn't close the door. I couldn't do it; it was too hard. Standing alone in the middle of the night on the side of the road, I looked up to the open sky. It was so black, I was so small, and I felt so lost and alone. But that moment of hesitation allowed my anger to rush back in, and that was all it took. The tears started to fall. I wouldn't, I couldn't, I shouldn't let this happen to me. I reached up to wipe the tears away. As my left hand brushed over my face where Paul struck me my right hand dropped the envelopes into the mailbox.

TWENTY-ONE

Dear Dead Dad:
It's Paul, again.

I am alone here in room 127 of the Atlas Mini-Storage. Alone. I had better get used to it.

Once I left Johanna's house, I hit the gas hard enough to see if the Firebird would live up to its name and fly through the air. Then when it crashed into the ground, would the screeching sound of the metal open the way for the ball of fire? When I drove over the bridge just before getting on the interstate, I can't tell you how tempted I was just to turn right about twenty feet too early. I could fly off the edge of the bridge, crash, and burn.

I felt a thousand miles from myself as I drove around and around that night. I drove fast, wanting to break the speed of light. I wanted to hurl myself back in time. Then I could erase Johanna. And Carla. And Vickie. Maybe I could even go back in time far enough so I could talk to you and beg you not to leave.

I skipped school today, just like the day before

and the day before that. I can't face anyone there; I can barely stand myself right now. I went to work, getting that good hurt in my back, just like you used to have hanging hoods on the line. Let's share our pain: both the taking and the giving. I'm feeling little pain right now, thanks to the Stroh's Brewing Company; I'm feeling lots of pain right now, thanks to the United States Postal Service. Here's what went down. I had just walked in the door from work when the phone rang. I knew it was Johanna. Carla always came back and things were much worse; Johanna would come back to me.

The phone is a scary thing. It just sits there, but it controls you. It brings you good news; it brings you bad news. Most people use the phone to bring bad news, but some folks—like you, Dad—couldn't go to the trouble of even a phone call.

I let it ring again.

If it was Johanna, I knew exactly what I was going to say. I was going to say that I was sorry. I was going to say that it wouldn't happen again. I would tell her things would change.

And then it rang again.

I would tell her that everything was going to be okay. I would tell her that everything was actually going to be better. I would tell her that she was beautiful and that I wanted her and that I needed her. I would tell her these things, and things would be like they were before.

And then it rang again.

"Hello." I said it fast, wanting to find out who was on the other end.

"Bro, how are you feeling? We're missing you here at school." It was Brad.

"Everything's cool," I said.

"Really?" He sounded confused.

"It's over with Johanna." I couldn't hide it from him; soon everybody would know.

"Bro, what happened?"

"Nothing to say." While Brad entertained me with tales of the highs and lows of life with Kara, I knew there was nothing entertaining about my story, and nothing about it that I wanted to share with anyone. If I told Brad, I knew he would keep it secret, but why bother?

"Well, bro, you know that I'm here if you want to talk it out," he said. His voice was comforting, big and warm.

"It hurts like hell." I wondered if he could tell that I was lying. It didn't hurt like hell. Hell would be a vacation compared to this. "I mean, you know it's going to happen, right?"

"What do you mean?"

"It's like Springsteen says: '. . . *soon as you got something, they send someone to try and take it away.*' When you love someone, you know that it comes to this. There comes a time when they won't be there anymore. If you give them everything, when you lose them, there is nothing left."

"It hurts, I know."

"I gave her so much, and now I have nothing. Nothing!" I slapped my hands off the kitchen table.

"Sometimes things just don't work out." He seemed to have more sadness in his voice than me by this time.

"Like us going to Stanford together. Whatever happened to those plans?" I asked.

"Got sidetracked on the wrong road, I guess," he answered.

"More like I hit a dead end," I said, then said my good-byes and hung up the phone.

Dad, I started toward my room but noticed several large envelopes with my name on them that must have come in the mail while I was at work. I ripped open one of the envelopes and reached inside. It was filled with this mass of paper. Who would send me a bunch of junk? Then I saw the Baskin-Robbins bags. Then I saw the earrings. Then I knew. I dumped everything on the table—the mess I had made of my life lay in front of me. Before I could cry, I quickly stuffed it back in the envelope and brought it here for you. So now I am sitting with you and with Johanna all around me.

She is just a memory now, just like you. Just like you, Johanna is leaving me. Just like you, Johanna couldn't stand to be around me. I grabbed the packages and my keys, got some beer, and Firebirded over here to room 127 to drink away my pain. Just like you.

TWENTY-TWO

Paul should be here in about an hour. It has been three weeks, six days, and twelve hours since I let Paul leave my life. Every morning so far this week during spring break, he has come by the house right after my parents have left for work.

On Monday morning he simply sat in his car in the driveway with the windows open and the sounds of "Thunder Road" pouring out of the Bird. I looked down from my bedroom window, but I didn't go downstairs. I lay back in bed, the pillow pressed over my head, smothering out the music. On Tuesday morning he knocked on the door a few times, but I refused to answer. Again he sat in the driveway playing music for me for almost an hour, and again I resisted. When the music stopped, I finally peeked out of my window and saw a dozen roses lying on the driveway. I went downstairs, looked outside to make sure he wasn't still around. I retrieved the roses from the driveway, depositing them directly in the trash. On Wednesday morning it was more of the same: a knock on the door, more music, and more flowers left behind. With the flowers were the words to my favorite Springsteen song—"If I Should Fall Behind"—handwritten on a single sheet of white paper.

We said we'd walk together baby come what may
That come the twilight should we lose our way

If as we're walkin a hand should slip free
I'll wait for you
And should I fall behind
Wait for me

We swore we'd travel darlin' side by side
We'd help each other stay in stride
But each lover's steps fall so differently
But I'll wait for you
And if I should fall behind
Wait for me

Now everyone dreams of a love lasting and true
But you and I know what this world can do
So let's make our steps clear that the other may see
And I'll wait for you
If I should fall behind
Wait for me

On Thursday the knocking was softer, the music louder, and wrapped with the flowers was another copy of the Valentine's Day CD Paul had made for me and a handwritten note:

Dear Joha—
I'm not good with words, like you, but I am going to do my best here.
    I am sorry.
    I have told you that I am sorry, but you won't forgive me.

I can't say that I blame you, but I want another chance. A last chance.

I am so sorry.

I want you to forgive me.

I want you to kiss me.

I know I said these words before, but this time I promise not to go back on these words. I promise things will change. I promise that I will change. You don't need to change; you are as close to perfection as a person could be. But I want one more chance, one last chance. I promise that I will treat you better.

You are everything to me.

I wish I could tell you why I do the things I do, but I don't really understand myself. I know that sometimes I drink too much, but that is going to change.

I know sometimes I get angry with you, but that is going to change, too.

Everything is going to change.

Sometimes I remember how we used to be, and I can't believe how happy I was, being with you. I remember seeing you in the hallway and just smiling, thinking that you were mine and no one else's.

Me, this trash bag, this person who has nothing— no father, no future, no money, nothing except you. You are so smart and so beautiful. I was so lucky to be with you. Trash bags like me don't deserve people like you. You are too good for me, I know that; but I want you so much.

My anger shouldn't be directed at you, because

you are the only thing that makes me happy (okay,
you, the Bird, the Boss, and Brad, but you are the
only one that I can't live without).

I never talked with you about my father, but he
is the reason for everything that I am and that I am
not. He is the reason I listen to Springsteen. He is
the reason that I drive the Bird. He is the reason
for my anger.

My father left me when I was twelve years old. I
came home from school one day, and there was a note
on the table.

I can't talk about this; I've never talked about
this with anyone, not even Brad.

It is not like life was great when he was there.
But then I came home from school one day and there
was a note on the table, and he was gone.

He was gone.

The next time we heard about him was just as I
was about ready to start high school. We got the
word that he was dead. He killed me the day I came
home from school and there was a note on the table,
and then he killed me again when he crashed his car
and died on an interstate outside of Houston, Texas.

He left me with nothing.

He left me.

Do you understand now?

Three people have said they loved me, and all have
left me. My father left me for a bottle, my mother
left me for Jesus, and you left me because of me.

I want you so much.

I need to talk to you. I need to make things
right between us. I need to stop my guts from
hurting. I need to stop us from hurting.

Like I said, I'm not good with words, like you.
I'm not an A student, like you. I don't have a
father, like you. I don't have much of a future,
like you. I don't have any of the things that you
have, but I will do my best for you.

I promise you that things will change. That I
will change.

I promise that I will do better, that things will
be better between us.

I am so sorry.

I want you to forgive me.

I want you to kiss me.

Please, please don't leave me ever again—

Wait for me—

P

After I read the note, I crawled back into bed. I put the CD in
my Discman and my headphones on, spending most of Thursday in bed, in tears.

Downstairs on Friday morning, I heard my parents getting
ready for work. I don't go down to breakfast anymore. It is no
use: I swear there is smugness on my mother's face. I told her
only one truth: that I broke up with Paul. Everything else was a
lie, and she believed it all. She acts concerned, but I don't trust
her. I don't know what to believe or who to trust. At school, Mr.
Taylor wanted me to see one of the school counselors, but I kept

putting him off. All these people want to help me, but all I want is to be left alone, to stop hurting, and to stop falling apart. I've made a mess of my life, but to admit that to my parents or Mr. Taylor would hurt even worse. I'll get through this, somehow.

The idea of food holds no appeal for me, not even ice cream. In the three weeks, six days, and twelve hours since I broke up with Paul, I have barely slept or eaten. My clothes are starting to drop off me. At school, I saw Paul in the hallway, even though we did our best to avoid each other. We are a hundred miles apart inside those four walls. A week ago, the day before spring break, I walked by the cafeteria at lunch and saw him sitting there, holding court with Brad, Kara, and her crew. He was cracking jokes to the people around him, and I was not part of it; so I only heard the laughter. That used to be my laughter, and now it is gone.

I don't laugh at anything. All the pain I had in my face and my body has formed a solid mass of hurt in my heart, and I can't let it go. Thinking about Paul is like having a loose tooth: I can't help but jiggle it, no matter how painful it is. It is too tempting. It is like my mom's smoking: She knows better, but she can't resist. I guess I never understood that until now about how something—or someone—can take over your life.

I picked up the phone and dialed. I knew the number by heart.

"Hello." A sleepy voice said on the other end of the line.

"Hi, Pam, it's Books." I sat down on the floor next to my bed. "I need to talk with you."

There was a pause, just as there had been a pause in our friendship.

"Please, Pam, don't hang up . . . just listen." Somehow defying the laws of anatomy, more tears welled up from behind my eyes. Each morning I thought I had none left; each morning I was wrong.

"Johanna, I don't think—"

"Call me Books," I said.

"No, Johanna. Look, this isn't right." Pam said, sounding as if she was speaking through clenched teeth.

Pam, like everyone else in school, knew that Paul and I had broken up. Also, like everyone else in school, Pam was clueless as to the real reason. She had never said she was sorry; but then again, I had never really apologized for how I had treated her. It was time to start making things right.

"Pam, look, I'm sorry about what happened between us. Paul, he said these things about you, and I didn't know what to do," I confessed.

Silence on the other end of the phone. Pure, dark silence.

"And he made me choose. It was wrong for him to do that. I know that now and—"

"Listen, maybe he did make you choose; but think about it," Pam replied, no longer hiding her anger at me. "You still chose him. You chose to be with someone who told you lies about your best friend. Don't blame him, Johanna. It was your choice."

"Pam, you don't understand," I replied weakly, since I didn't really understand myself why Paul had been so insistent about me cutting Pam out of my life. I didn't understand why he would make me do such a thing, but mostly I didn't understand why I went along.

"I don't think you understand how much you hurt me. I was happy about you getting together with Paul." Pam spoke slowly. "Sure, I was a little jealous because I didn't have a boyfriend then and because I enjoyed spending time with you. I knew things would change between us, and I was okay with that. But the way you cut me out completely, that was just wrong."

"I know it was wrong, and I'm sorry." I was lying on the floor now: All of my energy was directed toward the phone; there wasn't enough left even to sit.

"It's okay, I'm almost over it," Pam said.

"I'm so glad to hear that. I need to talk with you about Paul. I don't know—"

"Wait a second, Johanna," Pam said sharply. "What I said is that I can forgive what happened between us, but I can't forget it. I can't go back to how things were. Those were your words to me. Don't you remember saying, 'you can't have a friendship based on what was.'"

"Please, Pam, I need someone to talk—"

"I don't want to be mean, but I just can't do this. I'm sorry you broke up with Paul, and I know you must be hurting; but I can't do this. Good-bye." As I listened to the dial tone I realized that Paul had cut me off from everyone but him, and now even he was gone.

I hung up the phone, walked over to the window, and started waiting. Looking down into the driveway, I knew Paul's car would be there soon enough, followed by a knock on the door. The first morning it was easy, but each day it grew harder to resist turning the knob.

The ringing of the phone interrupted my window vigil. Before my parents could pick up, I bounded across the room and hoped to hear only one voice.

"Johanna, what's up?" Kara asked, her voice tired and hoarse.

"Kara?" I hoped my surprise and disappointment were not obvious to her.

"Hey, kid, are you okay?" she continued.

"Fine," I said. I lied.

"Really? That's not what I hear." She knew better.

"Did Paul ask you to talk to me?" I asked her, not really wanting to know the answer.

There was silence for a few seconds before Kara spoke. "Your friend Pam just called me out of the blue. She said you were really upset and that you needed to talk to someone."

"That was nice of her, but you didn't need to call. I'm okay." I hadn't talked with Kara in almost a month. I would see her at school, but she was either with her friends or with Brad. I knew that in the breakup, Paul got custody of them as a couple. It was understood.

"I don't know how you ever got away with that thing we did last Christmas," Kara said, then laughed.

"What do you mean?"

"You are such a lousy liar. Maybe your parents buy your bull, but don't try to sell it here," Kara said. "Now, how about telling me the truth, and nothing but the truth."

"It hurts like hell. I can't imagine anything hurting worse than this." Just saying it out loud to someone else made me feel better.

"I've been there," Kara said, although I didn't know how much she knew. I also didn't know how much I could, would, or should tell her.

"I was fine the first few days, but that must have just been shock. That wore off fast." I was speaking quickly, my words falling over each other. "Every morning I tell myself that today is the day that it won't hurt anymore. Then it hits me. Sometimes the pain starts the second my feet hit the floor. For so long I wanted to be with Paul. I hurt so bad wanting him. Then we were together, and now . . ."

"I'm so sorry," Kara said. She meant it, but I think she was letting me catch my breath.

"I guess I understand now why you and Brad always get back together again. It just hurts too much to stay apart."

"Well, the making up part is nice," Kara said, then laughed.

I wanted to laugh, only because I hadn't in so long; but my mind was racing and my tongue was loose. "If I can keep it together on the way to school, it is really not much of an accomplishment. It is only delaying the inevitable. Sometimes I make it onto the school bus. I sit near the front, bury myself in a book, and try not to look out the windows; but I never can resist. Every car that drives by I hope is a black Firebird."

"What happened between the two of you?" Kara asked.

It was my turn to pause and to lie again. Lying and crying were my two best talents now.

"I don't know." The fact that Kara asked I hoped meant she didn't know the truth, which was too shameful and too embarrassing to ever speak.

"Are you sure you don't want to tell me?" Kara said.

I ignored questions of history, focusing instead on biology. "It feels like the muscle that is my heart is actually torn. I'm limping along as best as I can."

"Well, you had better get that heart mended soon."

"I can't stand this, but I can't go back to him. Which hurt is the worst?"

"I don't know, Johanna, only you can decide that," Kara said. "But I know that you two had better get together."

"And why is that?" I asked.

"The prom is coming up, and I want you and Paul to go with us. That just seems right."

"The prom? That sounds so formal and normal," I said, amazed at how easy I still launched into Paulspeak.

"Well, I got to thinking about it. This would be my last chance to really hang out with all of my high school friends," Kara explained.

"That makes sense," I said, knowing that sadly, this was not something I could relate to, although I hoped to do better in this regard next year. Maybe I couldn't repair my friendship with Pam, but that experience taught me a hard lesson about making, and breaking, friendships.

"But mostly, it's about Brad," she continued, more seriousness in her voice than I was accustomed to hearing. "I just got to thinking about him and got all goofy sentimental like he does."

"Why is that?" I asked her. Kara and sentiment didn't sit well together.

"I don't know. I got to thinking about what happens in five years when I'm sitting around with a bunch of friends and we are talking about proms, and I say that I never went, because I thought it was all so stupid. I thought I might regret not going, just like I feel bad about fighting with Brad so much, like we did last year when we went to the prom."

"Really?"

"That was such a mess. We shared a table with Paul and that girl he was seeing, Carla. They started fighting, but that is all in the past, right?"

"I guess," I said without much conviction.

"Okay, now let me tell you the truth," Kara laughed. "I want to go to the prom to have one last chance to shock everyone and get their attention."

"Kara, I don't understand you. You are so beautiful and—"

"And Johanna, I don't understand you; you are so smart—"

"It's not the same thing." I smiled at Kara's transparent attempt to make me feel better about myself.

"And why is that?" Kara asked.

"For one, all girls want to be pretty. Do you think all the girls at Pontiac West dream about being in honors physics? Most of us would kill to look like you," I explained.

"What you don't know about other girls is a lot," Kara said.

"What do you mean?" I asked.

"It's not a contest, Johanna," Kara replied. "I just think that everybody wants what they don't have."

Before I had a chance to reply to Kara's insight, I was interrupted by my father shouting up the stairs, "JoJo, we're leaving!" I yelled out an acknowledgment, then pressed my ear against the phone again.

"Look, what matters is you and Paul getting back together," she said firmly.

"Paul and I—"

"I know, but let me tell you something, Johanna. I've been through this with Brad, and it just isn't worth it. I wish I could have back all the time that we spent fighting."

"You don't understand; it's not like that."

"I guess I can't understand, because I don't know what happened, and you don't want to tell me. If you want to tell me what is really going on, I'll listen."

"I don't know what to do," I replied, then lapsed into silence, which Kara respected.

"What does your heart say is the right thing?" Kara finally asked.

"I don't think my heart knows what the right thing is anymore."

Kara paused and spoke to me the way I wished my mother

would talk with me, rather than speak at me or question me. "Johanna, the heart always knows."

What I couldn't tell Kara was that my heart knew, but it knew too much. It knew that I loved Paul, and it knew that I hated him. It knew that I wanted to be with him again, and it knew that I had cried tears that said never again.

I heard the sound of the garage opening and closing; my parents were off to work, but somehow I figured that I would have a harder and more stressful day than both of them.

"Kara, look, I've got to go. Thank you for calling me; this was so sweet." I wished I could send her a huge hug through the phone.

"Thank your friend Pam," Kara explained.

"I will, but you saved me again," I said as I heard my parents driving away.

"Well, if you are drowning and you want to get saved, you've got to reach out, know what I mean?" Kara said. "I'll talk to you later, kid."

I hung up the phone, and then sprinted over to the window. Minutes that seemed liked hours passed until I heard the sound of the Bird coming down the street, then turning into the driveway.

Paul got out of the car, leaving his door open, filling the air with the sounds of "Thunder Road." He went around to the passenger-side door—my door—and opened it as well. He reached into the backseat, emerging with a rolled-up white sheet. I pressed myself up against the window as Paul unrolled the sheet over the hood of the Bird, holding down the edges with what looked like pints of ice cream, Baskin-Robbins chocolate chip no doubt.

CLIMB IN was written in big black letters.

As I cleared the tears from my eyes I heard the sound of Paul knocking on the door. But unlike the last four days, he didn't stop after a few tries. I moved from the bedroom to the top of the stairs. I sat there feeling my heart beating under my black T-shirt, beating, it seemed, in time with Paul's slow, steady, and soft knocking on the door.

My senses were overloading: the sounds of Springsteen spilling out into the March morning, the knocking at the door, the beating of my heart, the sound of Kara's voice, and the memory of Paul's laughter. I retreated briefly into my room and grabbed Paul's note and reread it, even though I had read it so many times that I had it almost memorized. The knocking continued as I started walking down the stairs. Kara wasn't an honors student, but she was smarter than me. The heart always knows.

I opened the door and let Paul back into my life.

"Joha, I am so sorry," Paul said, his hands stretched out before him. "So sorry for what happened between us."

"Paul, I need to hear it."

He wrapped his arms around me. His chin was resting again where it belonged, on my shoulder. "I am sorry for hurting you."

I squeezed him tight, hoping to force the words out of him. "For hitting me?"

He took my hands from around him and kissed them both, then kissed my forehead. The last time I was this close to him, his hands were slamming into my face; now his mouth was moving over the same place. "Joha, that will never happen again."

"Promise?" I asked. I needed to hear it again.

"I swear to you. Like I said in my note to you. Things are going to change."

I couldn't move; he was holding me so tight, our bodies were morphing together. They were resuming their natural shape. A hole had been created, but we were filling it in again. "Never again?" I said, fighting back tears.

"Never."

"You hurt me so much," I said, the memory of that night and all the nights of tears afterward.

"That's in the past. That never happened." He pressed my star-shaped earrings into my hands. "Joha, you are my star. I want you to have these back. I want you to take me back. I don't want to hurt anymore."

"I know Paul, I know," I said. I wanted to push all of the hurt out of his body, take it into mine. I wanted to take away all of his pain, all that hurt that spilled out in his note to me.

He lifted my glasses off, setting them on a table by the door. I didn't fight him. "I know I hurt you by what you saw me do."

He kissed over the top of my eyes.

"I know I hurt you by what you heard me say."

He kissed below both my ears.

"I promise I won't hurt you again, Joha."

He kissed me on the lips.

"I promise I just want to make you feel good and laugh."

He kissed the top of my throat.

"Everything is going to be okay. I need you so much."

He lifted my T-shirt up. I helped him pull it over my head. My face was flushed, my breathing was heavy, and my body was tingling.

"But mostly I hurt your heart," Paul said softly. He reached behind me, closing and then locking the door. "Let me kiss it and make it better."

TWENTY-THREE

"I am not wearing a tux!" Paul's voice boomed over the table and spilled into the rest of Santi's. It was two days before the prom, and the argument between Kara and Paul raged on.

"You can't wear a Springsteen T-shirt and torn blue jeans to a prom," Kara pleaded.

"I'll wear a tux once in my life, when they plant me six feet down in the brown ground. Let them get their deposit back from me, then," Paul was smiling, and that made me happy.

"Look, I don't care if it is pink or blue or purple, but you gotta wear one," Kara insisted. "Everyone else will be wearing one. You wore one last year."

"First off, I don't want to talk about last year. Second, I've changed. Third, since when did Brad and I do anything that anyone else did? Woman, have you not been walking this Earth with us for four years?" Paul looked around the table for an answer to his rhetorical question.

"Brad, tell him what you think," Kara said, kissing him on the cheek.

Brad started to sink under the table. "I think I would rather be anywhere else in the world than in the middle of this conversation." Everyone laughed.

"Johanna, help me out here, kid!" Kara said.

I took a big sip of my Coke to stall for time. "It's not my prom."

You guys decide, and let me know." I already knew what I was going to wear: that blood-red sleeveless gown Kara wanted me to buy last December. My arms were bruise free; Paul had kept his word.

"Another thing, I want a limo," Kara pressed on to the second point of contention.

"A limo is lamo. A limo is lemon. A limo is a no-go," Paul said as he waved his keys in front of Kara's face. "We fly in on the wings of my Firebird."

"No, I want the two of you in tuxes, and I want to be in a limo!" Kara sat back in the booth, her pouting cherry-red lips jutting out like a cliff.

Brad reached over and kissed Kara. "We'll work something out."

"It just doesn't make sense," Paul said, tapping the table with his finger. "You rent the limo, you rent the tux, you buy the tickets, you buy the dress, buy the haircuts, and then you puke over all of it drinking bad punch spiked with cheap wine." Even Kara had to laugh at that.

"So what are you guys doing after the prom?" Brad asked, trying to change the subject.

Paul pulled his glasses down his nose and stared at each one of us. His voice got very serious, very slow and solemn. "As you know, Bradley, the senior prom is an important time, not just in the life of the high school student, but the whole family. It is really a family affair."

"What are you saying?" Kara asked, scratching her cherry-red-streaked hair.

"What I am trying to say, my diva darling, is this night isn't just about Johanna and me." Paul reached his hand under the table and rubbed his right thumb between my legs. "What I am saying is after the prom, Johanna and I will be visiting the grandparents."

The Coke spit out of my mouth and nose all over Kara's dress, while my face turned even redder than her dress, lips, hair, or nails.

Kara got out of the Firebird first, getting her camera ready to capture the image of Paul and Brad stuffed into their tuxedos, standing in front of the Auburn Hills Country Club. Brad looked great; he could wear a potato sack and look good. Paul relented to Kara and was wearing a tux, albeit one that he and I purchased at the Salvation Army last night.

"We look like penguins out of water!" Paul complained as he reluctantly stood next to Brad to pose for a picture.

"Except penguins don't wear Converse high-tops or wrap-around sunglasses," Kara said, snapping the picture of Paul in all his accessorized glory.

"You just said I had to wear a tux, you didn't say anything about the other parts of my wardrobe," Paul said, his laughter filling the parking lot. "The shoes and the shades are black, which is very formal."

"Everybody will be staring at us," Kara said as we all walked toward the door.

"You're not one to talk, baby," Brad said, taking the camera from Kara, then quickly snapping photos of her, which she willingly posed for. No one was going to notice Brad, Paul, or me with Kara in our group.

Kara had dyed her hair platinum blond and painted her lips and nails the deepest shade of red I've ever seen. It defied the color spectrum. The bright white dress wasn't from any formal store intended for prom night. It was a cross between something from Victoria's Secret and a wedding dress. As I watched the parade of short black cocktail dresses followed by the long, flowing dark blue gowns file into the country club I knew that Kara, per usual, had smoked them all.

We handed off our tickets and walked inside. Paul had the DJ in his sights in just a few seconds. Paul told me he would get a Springsteen song played and vowed to stage a sit-down strike—in honor of his great-grandfather—in the middle of this dance floor if the DJ wouldn't play at least one of the songs.

While Paul was cutting up with the DJ and Kara was off with Jackie and Lynne taking photos, and having their photos taken, Brad and I sat at the table, both of us unmoved by the dance music pumping around us.

"So tell me what happened last year with Paul and Carla?" I asked Brad. Paul never wanted to talk about Carla, so I stopped asking; but I never stopped wanting to know.

Brad took a sip of water. "Don't know much about that, Chief."

A small voice in the back of my head was saying "Shut up, Johanna; let it go," but I pressed on. "Really?"

"Chief, you're one of the smartest people I know. Smarter than me, smarter than most of the people in this room." Brad reached across the table and grabbed my hands, then stared me down. "The smart thing is to just let it go. You can't change the past. All of us had a terrible time last year at this thing. Just let that go. It's history," Brad said with finality, and then motioned for Kara to come over the table.

I looked at Brad, searching those kind eyes for an answer, then I realized that he and Kara had given me the whole answer, and so had Mr. Taylor. When you're writing a first draft of history, mistakes will happen. Maybe the test of character Mr. Taylor talked about wasn't just about overcoming mistakes, but about forgiving them. I needed to let all of it go.

When we first walked into the prom, I saw Mr. Taylor and his wife standing by the front door. I wanted to go up and say hello, but I was still afraid and embarrassed. I could only hope that Mr. Taylor would forgive me for the way I'd cut him off. I could tell that he badly wanted to help me earlier this year, but I couldn't admit to him that someone he thought was so smart and mature was acting so stupid, all in the name of love. I wanted him to think that I could handle anything. Just because I had learned that I couldn't didn't mean my favorite teacher had to know.

"Ready to dance?" Paul asked, rubbing his hands gently on my back. I had been so lost in my thoughts I was unaware that Paul had sneaked up behind me.

"Of course, but there's no Springsteen playing," I said as we moved toward the dance floor.

"Just wait," Paul said. His face broke out in a huge smile of pride when "If I Should Fall Behind" boomed over the speakers. We were about the only two dancing as Bruce sang.

"How did you get the DJ to play it?" I asked.

"The jacket of the CD I gave him was filled with titles of top forty crap." Paul was smiling. "But every track was this song; so no matter what he picked, we were getting this."

Paul and I were spinning small circles on the dance floor. As he and I moved together I tried to let the music take me over, but I couldn't shut my mind down. I wanted to be perfect: the perfect student, the perfect editor, the perfect girlfriend, and the perfect lover. But even if I was learning more every day that I couldn't be perfect, this moment was.

As we danced I felt memories sweep over me. The first time we kissed sitting in the Firebird. The first time we danced at Jackie's party. The first time we made love at my grandparents' house that December night. I was losing control to the moment and how it connected with every other moment in my life. If the music stopped right now, if I had to decide my life right at this moment, I would choose to spend it with Paul. My parents, my plans and their plans, and maybe even my potential, be damned; this is where I wanted to be. I didn't need a crystal ball; I just wanted a mirror to reflect this image forever. My whole life was happening now, spilling out in front of me. There was no hitting and no crying; there was no shouting and no screams; there was only this moment. I wished the song would never end and the sun would never rise.

When the song ended, and my dream was denied, I wouldn't let go of Paul. I wouldn't let go of this moment.

"Joha, what's wrong?"

The tears tasted as sweet and fresh as ice cream. My mouth was savoring the sweetness; it had no time to waste uttering mere words.

Another song started, the music boomed and bodies around us started to shake to the faster beat; but I didn't move. I wouldn't let go of this moment.

"Joha, what's wrong?" Paul asked, bending down and cupping my chin in his hands. I took off his sunglasses so I could see his eyes. But I didn't answer; there were no words.

"What's wrong?" Paul leaned into me, our faces just inches away from each other. "What do you want?"

The answer was as obvious as it was old. "I want you to kiss me."

TWENTY-FOUR

Dear Dead Dad:

I am listening to *Darkness on the Edge* of Town by the Boss over and over again. The song "Adam Raised a Cain" bores into my mind, especially the line "you inherit the sins, you inherit the flames." I have been thinking about you a lot these past few days. I graduated from high school last week. Mom gave me two things for my graduation. One was her mother's Bible. Exactly what I needed.

I don't think you would even know Mom now. I don't remember even going to church when you lived here, but now it is her life. She only goes twice a week but talks about it all the time. She sits in our trailer all day watching the Christian TV station. She tells me she prays for me. If only that made a difference. I guess she thinks Jesus will protect me, although he did a lousy job of protecting her. Protecting her from you.

The other gift was a gold watch. Another thing I needed not one bit. I guess I can use the watch to time my life, ticktock as time slips by and I die here day by day.

I am going to apply to the community college. I think I have enough money to pay if I can stay working forty hours this summer, eight hours a day, five days a week. You used to work eight hours a day, sleep for eight, and drink for eight. A perfectly divided life.

Sometimes you took time away from your drinking to smack Mom around. I always wondered how you could treat her that way. How could you hit someone you loved? You never hit me. I guess you didn't love me, did you Dad? Because if you loved me, you wouldn't have left. You would have stayed around and beat the shit out of me.

You never hurt me with your hands. You did it with just eighteen words.

Let's take a walk, not down Thunder Road, but down memory lane. I am twelve years old. I do well at school. I am well-liked. I get picked first or second to play on the sports teams, and everybody seems to think that I have some potential. I come home one day on the bus to a nice house, not a trailer. It is February. I have a stack of Valentine cards. One of the girls who sits behind me, Cheryl Lindsay, likes me. I remember that when I got off the bus, I was eating a peanut-butter cookie from a party that day.

Your Firebird wasn't in the driveway when I got home, which surprised me, since I remember you got laid off over Christmas and never went back to work, so you were around a lot, at least during the day. I

knew you would be home by two in the morning. That is
when the shouting started. I didn't know what that
was all about, and I didn't really care. I had a
house; I had a mother; I had a father. I had a life.

So I walk in the door. Mom had a job then, so she
was gone. I knew what I was supposed to do; I did it
every day. I would come home, sit in front of the
TV, and wait until she got home around four.

So I walk in the door that day, my breath
smelling of peanut-butter cookie. I don't see anyone
in the house, and that is okay. It is quiet, and I
welcome it. Sometimes you and Mom fought so loud, it
scared me. It scared me when you hit her. I wanted
to protect her, but I was too small to do anything.
But I guess I also wasn't really sure it was wrong.
How could it have been wrong if she never left? I
thought it was normal. I thought everyone's family
was like this.

So I walk in the door that day and put my books
down. Then I see a note on the table. Sometimes Mom
would leave me notes if she was going to be late. I
remember when I first started coming home from school
that you would leave me things like candy or baseball
cards. You would write a short note, in that terrible
handwriting of yours, saying you loved me. That day
the note on the table is in your handwriting, but
there is no candy. I've kept the note; I never even
gave it to Mom. She thinks you just vanished without
even a good-bye; I know better.

I am sitting here in room 127 of the Atlas Mini-

Storage. My breath doesn't smell of peanut butter,
it reeks of the hops, yeast, and other ingredients
mixed together by my friends at the Stroh's Brewing
Company in Detroit, Michigan. They were your
friends, too. Next to me is my high school diploma.
Do you know what this diploma means? It means that
my days of being a child are over; I am a man now.
But you already gave me that diploma when I was
twelve years old. I wonder if I should have that
framed, too. It means more to me than this diploma.

I am sitting here in room 127 of the Atlas Mini-
Storage looking at these two pieces of paper. The one
I worked for; the other was a gift. Your good-bye
gift to me. Let me read it to you, just in case you
forgot the note that you wrote to your twelve-year-
old son. Just in case you forgot the final words you
ever communicated to me. Just in case you forgot the
words you used to graduate me at age twelve from being a child to being this pathetic drunken trash bag
that writes to you pretending that you are still
alive. Let me read it to you now, dead man—

> Dear Paul—
> I am leaving, please tell your mother.
> Everything is going to be okay.
> Trust me,
> Dad

"Johanna, I know exactly how you feel." I looked over at Jackie, my eyes focusing on her mouth, which had uttered those magic words.

Lynne adjusted the strap of her too-tight black tank top, then slugged back another gulp of what seemed like her tenth cup of coffee. "I feel that way all the time about my parents."

"You do?" I sniffled, trying to suck it up and not make a scene here in Ann Arbor, the home of the University of Michigan and the mecca of the hip and well-read.

With Paul working almost all the time, I was at loose ends. At Kara's graduation party I overheard Kara, Lynne, and Jackie talking about a road trip to Ann Arbor. Just like I did that day in the car with Paul, I summoned up my courage and prepared for rejection when I asked if I could join them. To my surprise, they seemed happy to have me come along.

"Lynne, what about you?" I asked. Lynne looked up, her blue eyes shining brighter than her perfect smile.

"My parents think they're flawless. I think that is the saddest and the worst part of it." Lynne answered, almost in a whisper. I could barely hear her with the alt rock blaring over the speakers and the muddled conversations of "tramps like us" who had jammed into Starbucks.

"Mine, too, although they have a perfect system," I added.

The complaints departed from my mouth with surprising ease. "My father was a marine, so my house is very rigidly organized. It's like on TV. You know how they talk about good cop, bad cop. My house is more like evil genius general, bad bitch lieutenant."

"That's funny," Kara said.

"No, that's screwed up," Jackie said.

"That's my life." I rolled my eyes for emphasis. "They just won't let go."

"I wonder if graduating is going to change that?" Lynne asked no one in particular.

"God, I thought I was the only one." I almost shouted the words; sharing the pain of my parents made me ecstatic. I had been telling them about my mother's once-a-week rule and all the other roadblocks thrown on my path to Paul.

"My mom has two faces." Jackie was on a roll as she pulled out a clove cigarette from her purse, bouncing it on the table to the rhythm of her speech. "She's like always telling me to stand up for myself, be strong. Be strong, she says, except when it comes to obeying her. She's always yelling at me for stuff, and then if I talk back, she just yells louder."

Jackie was living my life. We had been in the same school for three years on opposite sides of the social spectrum, yet we still occupied the same emotional space. Mr. Edwards would tell me the laws of physics wouldn't allow it, but Jackie and I were living parallel lives.

"At least she just yells," Lynne said in a tone as cold as the ice coffee I had been sipping for the past hour. "My mom never yelled; she just used to hit."

"Lynne, I'm so sorry." It was all I could say. I didn't want to talk about hitting at all. I couldn't talk about it; I had to hear about it.

"Sorry?" Lynne looked at me with surprise. She pushed the

blond hair from in front of those baby blues and shook her head. "Johanna, when you say you're sorry, you make it sound like you pity me or like it is my fault. That's wrong on both accounts."

"I was just—" I started.

"It's not so bad anymore, but every now and then. Every now and then." Lynne had no emotion in her voice whatsoever.

"What did you do?" I asked, needing the answer badly.

"I hope you told them off," Jackie jumped in, ready to take on the world. "Got in her face and told her to knock it off or else."

"You sure can be dumb sometimes," Lynne said, causing laughter all around. She was wrong: I had underestimated Kara and her friends; they were all very smart in ways I only hope to achieve.

"What do you mean?" Kara asked.

"I'm just kidding, Kara, chill," Lynne said. "It is just that there is no 'or else.' I just told my mom that she wasn't going to hit me again. You gotta take a stand."

I sat back thinking about those words and savored my coffee while the three of them launched into a discussion about their post–high school plans. They chatted about maybe finding second jobs and then getting an apartment together, but it seemed more talk than anything else. Finally Kara drew me back into the conversation.

"So what are you going to do after you graduate? Should we save a room for you?" Kara asked.

"I'll probably go to college," I said, like I was ashamed.

"Johanna, you are still such a bad liar," Kara said, then laughed. "You know you'll go to college, probably a school like Stanford, all expenses paid. I would love something like that."

I laughed and let down my guard. "I don't think I'll be going to Stanford. I want to go to Columbia in New York City."

"Does Paul know that?" Kara asked, raising her eyebrow just like she had seen me do in reaction to one of Paul's bad puns.

"No, I haven't told him," I confessed. "Or my parents. They want me to go to school here. This is hard stuff to figure out, especially since I don't have anyone to talk with about it."

I finally shutup and chewed my thumbnail, washing it down with a big swig of ice-cold coffee. There would be no chance for a refill as they finally turned the lights off on us.

"Johanna, I told Lynne and Jackie that you were the smart one. That was a really dumb thing to say," Kara said softly.

"What did I say?" I asked, the tension in my voice obvious to all.

"You said you didn't have anyone to talk to about this," Kara said, putting her hand on my shoulder. "You have us."

I locked on to those words: "You have us." Then I remembered what Jackie had said earlier in the evening: "I know exactly how you feel." I think I had been waiting my whole life to have friends who would say those things to me. I missed Pam, but this was different. This was belonging to a group and not feeling left out, like Pam and I often did. This feeling of being part of something other than me and Paul was so new to me. My parents always told me that my grades were outstanding, but tonight I didn't feel like I was standing out at all.

The cool of the evening and the coming morning never felt more soothing than when we walked outside. The street, although less crowded, was the same as when we had entered the Starbucks hours ago, but something was different. Looking at my reflection in the Starbucks window, and then looking at Kara, Jackie, and Lynne, it felt like an earthquake rumbled inside of me. I could actually feel my life change; it was a visible shift.

TWENTY-SIX

"Just where do you think you are going, young lady?" my mother asked me as I stood next to the refrigerator drinking a glass of juice. I was dressed up, wearing a short white sleeveless dress that Kara and her friends helped me pick out.

"Paul is coming over to pick me up around noon," I replied, and then let out a loud yawn. I tried to sleep most of the way home from Ann Arbor, but the conversation with Lynne, Kara, and Jackie continued during the drive back, and then later at a twenty-four-hour diner. All the while I was talking and laughing I was also planning for this morning.

"You're seeing Paul today and Wednesday." My mother punctuated her statement with a smoke ring, as though she expected me to jump through it like a trained seal.

"I think I'll probably see Paul today, tomorrow, the day after, and the day after that, and then all next weekend." I stated it as fact, not a matter of dispute.

"Since when do you think you get to set the rules around here, Johanna?"

"I want to talk about these rules." I sat myself down at the table, getting comfortable for some uncomfortable times in the making. All I could think about was what Lynne had said: "You gotta take a stand."

"There is nothing to discuss." My mother started out the

door. My father sat there, solid as a stone. This had become the pattern of their interaction with me since February. My mother would question and try to control me; but if I didn't respond, she would just throw up her hands in frustration. She held back her trump card of "I told you so," while my father said very little. He cared, but I guess he couldn't find a way to break through my defenses, and I didn't make it easy.

"Mom, you have to be fair," I yelled after her.

She pivoted on her heel. "Your father and I are being very fair about this. We told you that you could see Paul twice a week during the summer. You don't think that is fair?"

"No, that's not fair at all."

"I don't like your tone," my mother said, her voice raised. "Why do you think you can talk to me like this? Is this how your precious Paul talks to his mother?"

"I just don't like your rules," I said back to her. I didn't want to talk to my mother like Paul talked to his mom, but I wanted her off my back. Same end, different means.

My father, as usual, was lying in wait, silent, acting like the reserve battalion.

"You live here, you obey our rules. What is so hard about understanding that?"

"I will obey reasonable rules, but these aren't reasonable. They aren't fair."

"I guess we just disagree on what is fair," my mom said, again walking out of the room—signifying that in her mind, the conversation was over and I was dismissed.

"Mom, I want to talk about this," I said. My voice was shaking, which made sense because my whole body was one raw nerve.

My father got up, looked past me, and followed my mother

into the family room. I had been writing this speech in my head as I tossed and turned in bed for those few hours last night.

"Really?" My mother smiled as if I were amusing her.

"Really," I shot right back at her, and followed them until I stood in front of them. I was fully clothed, but I felt naked because I was going to tell them how I felt about everything. It was a few weeks late, but it was Independence Day. Time for the fireworks.

"I do everything you ask of me, and I always have. You have pushed me to succeed, and I have. Those things matter to you, and they matter to me." I paused to catch my breath and continued to summon my courage.

"You just listen one second—" my mother started.

"No, it's time for you to listen." I watched her visibly recoil; my father's eyes remained cold. "I've thought about this for a long time. I want to be able to go out with Paul, not once a week, not twice a week, but as much as I want. I'm sorry you don't like Paul, but I do."

My mother was shaking her head. "Listen, Paul is—"

"This isn't about Paul. This is about me." I cut my mother off again. "You've told me for as long as I can remember that I was smart. If I am so smart, then give me control over my life. I'm not saying that I shouldn't have to obey any rules, but you need to ease up on me. You need to let me live my life. *My* life."

My mother sighed. "Explain to me why this young man with his loud car, dirty clothes, and long hair is so important to you. You're going places, but he'll be here forever. Can you tell me why he matters so much, because your father and I don't understand it?"

"Because I love him." I didn't even stumble over the word *love*.

My mother laughed at me. Not a chuckle, not a giggle, a full-fledged laugh. She could have pulled every hair out by the root and not hurt me any more than she did with that laughter. "Johanna, you are too young to be so involved with anyone, especially someone like Paul."

"What does that mean?" I asked angrily, not ignoring her insult.

"Don't you think your father and I know what is going on?" she asked.

I took a deep breath, hoping my lies hadn't been discovered. "I don't think you care."

"JoJo, of course we care. We want the world for you," my father said, breaking his silence. "Your grades are going down. You don't talk with us. Your teachers are concerned."

"How would you know?" I asked.

"Mr. Taylor called us. There are a lot of people who care about you," my father said.

"People other than Paul," my mother said. "Just because the two of you have shared some kisses doesn't mean he loves you or that you really love him. You just—"

"I knew you were going to say that," I said. I wanted to knock the cigarette out of her hand and the smirk off her face and tell her how I had shared not just my lips with him, but my whole body. How I had shared a bed with him, too, but this wasn't about anger. This was about my life becoming mine first and theirs second. "Maybe you're right, Mom. Maybe I don't know what that word means, but let me decide that. Let me define it. You need to trust me."

"Of course we trust you; why would you say such a silly thing?"

"You say that, but you don't really mean it," I shouted back at her.

My mother looked at my father; they both sighed. They looked at me as a child, but I wanted to be a woman. To Paul, I was. I had changed, and they hadn't even noticed.

"Honestly, where do you get all these ideas?" my mother asked me. She didn't think I was serious. "Is it Paul? It must be because you're too smart to say such stupid things."

I wasn't backing down. "I've been thinking about this for a long time."

"See what happens with just one day in Ann Arbor," my father chimed in. "If this is what you learn these days at U of M, then maybe we had better send Jo someplace else."

"Don't worry about that!" My tongue was running two laps ahead of my brain, but I was in no mood to even out the race. "I'm not going to Michigan; I'm going to Columbia."

"Oh, really?" my mother asked, raising her eyebrows.

"I've decided," I said, crossing my arms. "So you see, you won't have to worry about Paul much longer. He'll be in California, and I'll be in New York."

"How do you think you'll pay for that?" my father, the big bear of the practical, asked.

"I'll get a job this summer and after school next year," I answered firmly.

"Seems you've made yourself a few plans, doesn't it? You think that this is all your decision. We've made plans for you. We thought it was what you wanted, too," my mother said.

"It's my life," I said. "It's *my* life, and I want it back. I want it back starting now."

"Oh, let me tell you something, Johanna Marie—"

"No, let me tell *you* something. I don't care anymore. You can set rules, and I can break them, or you can learn to respect *my* decisions. But I'm not going to fight with you the rest of the summer and all of next school year about Paul. Do you hear me?" I shouted at her.

"You won't give me an ultimatum, young lady."

I smiled at her, trying to capture her smirk and reflect it back, trying to force that bitter medicine down her throat. "Well, it seems like I just did."

I wanted to vomit, I was so scared. I needed Kara, Jackie, and Lynne here. I needed Paul here. But I also needed to do this for myself, by myself.

"Enough," my father said. He looked at me with those cold eyes. I don't think that my father really understood me, but he understood this.

"I'm going outside to wait for Paul," I said, starting toward the door.

"You will do no such thing!" my mother shouted, the veins on her neck bulging.

I just kept walking toward the door.

"Johanna Marie!" my mother's shout morphed into a screech.

"And I said, 'enough'!" I turned to see my father touching my mother's arm, those words directed at her, not me.

She pulled herself away from my father and started back at me. Her eyes were manic and her voice at full volume. "You will not talk to me like that! Johanna Marie, you get back over here right now or else—"

"Or else what?" I asked as I turned on my heel to face her, to confront her.

"Or else!" she shouted even louder now, then pointed her finger at me, bringing it within inches of my face.

I instinctively cringed. The muscle memory of Paul jamming his index finger hard into my shoulder overwhelmed me. "Get your finger out of my face!"

"Enough," my father repeated, but this time softer, this time aimed at us both. As I looked at my mother, I think we both instantly realized that a Rubicon had been crossed. She had lost control, and in doing so, her illusion of control was shattered. I was her daughter, but maybe she finally realized that it was my life to run, or ruin.

The screen door slammed behind me, and I never looked back.

Paul slowed the Bird down when he saw me standing outside at the end of my driveway, broiling in the July heat. I ran toward him. He gave me a huge hug, lifting me off the ground. Spinning me, spinning me in small circles just like we were dancing.

"Joha, you look great!" Paul's mouth was almost hanging open.

I took over on his open mouth, covering it with kisses. If my mother was watching, even better. The aftermath of the fight and the joy of Paul's hug was too much all at once. It was hot, but these tears were too heavy to evaporate in the steaming Sunday sun.

"Joha, what's wrong, baby?" Paul asked as we climbed into the Bird.

"I just had a big fight with my parents, with my mother," I said, talking through tears.

"What about?" Paul asked as we roared away from my house.

"Nothing," I said, then took a deep breath. "Everything."

"It's going to be okay." He pulled me close, and I buried my head in his shoulder.

"My mom was out of control, but my dad told her to leave me alone." I couldn't get the image out of my mind, maybe because I didn't understand it. "Why would he do that?"

"Maybe you showed him some of that marine toughness he's been grinding into you for years," Paul said, holding me even tighter now.

"I don't know how they stand each other. He's so in control of himself, but she just wants to control me." I felt goosebumps popping up on my lightly tanned skin.

"Hey, you're the science queen. Don't opposites attract?" Paul laughed. "Like us."

I laughed for the first time all day. "Maybe."

"So what's the fallout?" he asked as he wiped the tears from my eyes with his fingers.

"I don't know. Something happened between them, between them and me. It was ugly."

"And you're so beautiful; look at yourself," Paul said. "What's up with that?"

"We went shopping last night in Ann Arbor," I said. "We were out really, really late."

"You tired?" Paul asked as I collapsed against him.

"I just want to get to bed," I said. "Is your mom at church?"

"If it's Sunday, she's at church," Paul said with a smile.

"Well, maybe we could go visit the grandparents," I whispered.

"I think that could be arranged," Paul replied. I rocked back in his arms and studied his face. He had made some changes since graduating. It didn't look like he had shaved since getting his diploma, so a small growth of beard was forming. Just like I had memorized the multiplication tables, the laws of physics, and the design of the ceiling in my bedroom, I was committing every inch of his face to long-term-memory storage. I ran my fingers across his cheek, taking in the texture for the nights I would be alone without him.

"Paul, I'm going to get a job this summer," I said softly, unsure how he would react.

"I hope not working with crazy Kara and her kooky crew at the mall," Paul said.

I paused before answering, wondering why he had thrown in that dig at Kara. "I don't know where yet. I just need to save money for college."

"Let's celebrate!" Paul said as he reached behind the seat. He held the bottle of Stroh's, but I declined it with my eyes. He twisted off the cap and took a gulp. "I salute you!"

"No, don't do this." My voice was firm as I pulled away from him.

"No problem, Joha, I know my limit."

"Zero." I crossed my arms and pouted. "Promise me, Paul."

"That's not fair; it's just one—"

"Zero." I was becoming a clone of my father. Short answers, no discussion allowed.

"Damn it, Johanna," Paul said, sitting the beer in the cupholder, then slapping his hand against the dash. He roughly ejected the CD out of the player. He let up on the gas. We pulled off the interstate, and he turned the engine off. We sat there for a minute in total silence; the only sound was that of cars whishing by us at seventy-five miles an hour.

He reached into the back and grabbed the rest of the six-pack. He walked in front of the car, the open bottle in one hand and two bottles in the other.

"Paul, please don't be mad," I shouted at him through the open window, trying to avoid yet another terrible and bruising scene between us. "Paul, please—"

I didn't finish my sentence. Instead, I watched Paul pour the contents of each bottle on the ground, a beer river forming by the side of the Firebird. When he was finished, he leaned into the car, getting right in my face. I couldn't believe it; my body was tensing up, fearing the worst, fearing the past was about to repeat itself.

Instead, Paul put his hands gently on the side of my head, and then leaned in to kiss me.

"You're going to be working now," he said with a smile, one breaking out on my face as well. "You owe me five dollars for those beers."

TWENTY-SEVEN

Dear Dead Dad:
It's Paul, again and for the last time. I am writing
to say good-bye.

   I never got a chance the first time you left, so
here it comes.

   Good-byes are on my mind. I just watched Brad
drive out of my day-to-day life. So this is my last
letter to you. I'm done playing pretend with you.
I've grown up.

   One of the things we did in school was read
Hamlet. I got off a lot of good lines, so maybe my
teacher thought I didn't care about the play. It's
about this kid haunted by the ghost of his father. I
just wanted to kick Hamlet's ass, tell him to either
shit or get off the pot, make a decision already,
move on with your life. It's easy to watch someone
else's life crash and burn, harder to watch your own
accident up close. You need distance in your life.
So, listen: I am done being haunted by you.

   Brad left this fine August morning for
California. He invited me to drive with him, but I
couldn't leave Johanna alone for that long. Brad and
I met at Supreme, like we always do. He was well

into his third cup by the time I arrived. I grabbed
a white cup, filled it with black, and joined him.

"Well, bro, this might be the last time we sit at this table," Brad said, pushing the chair out for me. "The last time we'll drink this fine coffee. The last time we'll enjoy the fragrant secondhand smoke of Supreme Donut. The last time we—"

I interrupted. "The last time we'll hear you say 'this is the last time.'"

He laughed. "And the last time you will tell me not to talk about 'the last time.'"

I held the plain white coffee cup in my hands. It was mid-August and ninety degrees outside, but I felt a chill sliding around my spine. "Kara see you off?"

"Last night." The smile vanished from his face.

"Rough, huh?" I said, sipping my coffee. The weight of the mug was perfect.

"It was a scene. I didn't think it would be that way."

"Really?"

"I mean, we had broken up before; we knew this day was coming. She thinks I'll meet someone at school and forget about her. I know she'll meet someone here and forget about me."

"I don't think that is going to happen," I said, leaning back in my chair.

"It was like every other time we broke up, in some ways; but there were more tears and less screaming. This time, I think it's over for good."

"You'll stay in touch," I offered, tapping him on the shoulder with a light punch.

"We say that, but it won't be the same. She knows it. I know it."

"And I know it won't be the same with us. No more Supreme meetings, no double dates, just E-mail and phone calls. We'll be connected by nothing but wires," I said sadly.

"I have something to tell you," Brad said with seriousness in his voice that I rarely heard. We shared jokes, insults, and stories: We spoke of motion more than emotion. "I lied to Kara. She asked me if she was the first person that I ever loved. I lied to her; I told her yes. You are my best friend, Paul, and I love you for it. You got me through these past four years. You made me laugh and never let me down. I made a shitload of mistakes in high school, but being your friend wasn't one of them. I am always there for you—night or day, wrong or right."

"I know, bro. I know," I said. Brad's heart was huge: He would always protect me.

Brad smiled; but then he started to cry, although he was fighting it. "I can't cry because that would just create a sixth Great Lake right in the middle of Supreme Donut."

"Why do you care; don't you walk on water, anyway?" I cracked.

"I gotta get going." Brad swilled down the last drop of the Supreme substandard brew.

We walked out to his car. It was jammed full of his life. "You showed me the way." I kicked the tires on Brad's car for emphasis. "I'm gonna save my money, get good grades at the CC, and get into Stanford next fall. Start brewing the coffee. I'll be joining you in about a year."

"What about Johanna?" Brad asked as he opened the driver's-side door.

"What about her?"

"Is she coming, too?"

"I don't know what she is doing, and it doesn't matter. I gotta get out of this place. I'm going to change my life. You get that coffee ready."

Brad wrapped me in a bear hug. "I'm gonna miss you, bro."

He turned the engine on. "Check it out," he said as he pointed to the dash. On it was a picture of the four of us from the prom, pasted there.

"I have something for you," I told Brad as he climbed into his packed car.

"Man, don't do this now," he said with mock anger. "I don't have room for it!"

"You have room for this." I reached into my wallet. "Here."

"What is it?" he asked, slowly taking the object from me.

"Take it, damn it!" I yelled at him. I was losing it. I started walking toward the Bird, turning back to see Brad looking at my going-away gift.

Brad looked at the picture. It was a picture of you, Dad, my only one. It was all I could give him to let him know how much I valued his friendship. It was the last piece of you I could share with anyone.

So I said good-bye to Brad this morning, and it gives me the courage to say good-bye to you now. You are not all around me anymore. Like Brad, you are gone. He'll come back for the holidays; you will not. My life has changed. And I don't need you in it anymore.

You got to say it to me when I was twelve. I turn eighteen in two weeks, and it is my turn to say it to you. I am leaving you; everything is going to be okay with me, trust me.

TWENTY-EIGHT

"Thanks for coming," Kara said as I sat next to her in a booth at the Starbucks in the mall. Her eyeliner and her nose were both running.

"Any time," I answered.

"Jackie and Lynne, they're great; but I don't think they understand like you do," Kara said, the queen of cool was melting in front of me. "I shouldn't bother you with this."

"Like you told me, if you want to be saved, you got to reach out your arms," I said. She laughed, then squeezed my left hand.

"God, I miss Brad," Kara said. "You are so lucky that Paul didn't go with him."

"I know," I said, and slowly pulled my hand away from Kara. If she squeezed my hand again, I would be fine. But if she touched my arm under the long sleeve shirt I was wearing in the August heat, she might touch the bruise Paul made on my arm last night after we fought about how I wasn't spending time with him. Ever since I started working at the bookstore a month ago, we had been fighting too hard and making up too easy. The pain in my shoulder or wrist I could bear, but I knew I couldn't handle my heart breaking again. Paul had gone back on his word to change, and I had let him. We were both liars: Maybe we deserved each other.

"Why do you think Paul really didn't go to Stanford with Brad?

If he would have saved the money he spent on his car, on you, and on his friends, I'm sure he could have made it work," Kara said.

"I really couldn't tell you," I replied, the doubt in my voice giving way to more silence. This was the question that I had been trying to answer since December. It was such an easy question, so why was the answer so hard to understand? Did he really stay here because of me? Was it because he couldn't afford it? Could he have even gotten in with his grades? This was a riddle I never successfully solved, because I sensed there was a trick answer. I wanted to believe that he really stayed for me. But even then, as much as that flattered me, it had a downside. When he was frustrated at work or upset about something with his mom, I could almost hear the words dancing on the tip of his tongue or swelling up in his hands, ready to explode: "I stayed here for you; it is all your fault."

I smiled at Kara but could do nothing more than repeat myself. "I just don't know. Leaving home is scary."

"I know the answer," Kara said. "He didn't go, because it was too easy to stay."

"How do you know that?" I looked at Kara with a blank stare.

"I don't know Paul. I only know me," Kara said.

"You, afraid?" I asked.

"Oh, Johanna, you are so funny," Kara said, but she wasn't laughing. "Why do you think I keep getting back with Brad?"

I was mute. I knew better than to go back to Paul, but I did it anyway. The heart knows.

"And all those wild clothes?" Kara continued. "If you try to fit in and people reject you because they think you're stupid, that hurts a lot. So I guess I figured I wouldn't give them a chance. I would just be out there and make them feel stupid for not getting it."

"I never thought you were stupid," I lied.

"Yes, you did, and I don't blame you. I thought you were this stuck-up smart-ass. It doesn't matter, anyway. Nothing matters now that Brad is gone. I'm nothing without him," Kara said, her tears returning.

"Yes, you are something," I said softly.

"What is that?" she asked, barely managing a smile.

I smiled in return. "You are my best friend."

TWENTY-NINE

"Is this why they call it wearing your birthday suit?" Paul said, pressing his naked body up against mine. "Happy birthday to me, and happy anniversary to us!"

I laughed, then reached over to the small table to take another spoonful of the chocolate-chip ice cream. Paul had checked into the hotel room before me and put cartons of ice cream in the sink, the bathtub, and the ice bucket. Let others have champagne; I was in hog heaven.

"Corny!" I said.

"No, horny," Paul said as he moved down on the bed, pressing against me.

"Again?" I shot him the brow, which for some reason cracked us both up.

"What?" he asked with mock shock in his voice. "I told the people at the *Guinness Book* to be on standby because we were going for a new world record!"

"I think the people next door hate us already."

"They probably think we are praying, since you keep yelling 'Oh God,'" Paul joked.

"No, for laughing so loud," I said. "Anybody can do this, but only you make me laugh."

"Well, but not everybody can do it this good." He pushed out his lips in a major pout.

I kissed him. "Paul, you don't do it good. You're great."

He brushed his face against mine. "Nice of you to say, but without anyone else to compare me to, you don't have what you science types would call a scientific sample."

I pointed to one of the used condoms in the wastebasket near the bed. "Now, that's a sample."

That did it. We started laughing so much that we fell out of the bed, onto the hotel floor. Despite my best attempts, my schedule at the bookstore called for me to work both Wednesday nights and Sundays starting at noon. Since I lived in fear of my parents walking in on us at my house, Paul decided to post-celebrate his eighteenth birthday, and pre-celebrate our one-year anniversary at the Hilton on Telegraph Road, just outside of the city. We wouldn't spend the night, just a couple of hours; but it was enough.

As I crawled back onto the bed Paul reached over and grabbed his fatigues.

"I have a present for you," he said, reaching into the pocket of his pants.

"What is it?" I sat up on the bed and pulled the covers up in front of me.

"This is for you to wear at school next year." He kissed me, and then he handed me a small jewelry box. He smiled as he watched me drop the covers, and then I carefully started taking off the gift-wrap. I had started saving the paper again.

I opened the box. It was a beautiful, and very expensive, star-shaped necklace.

"This is so beautiful." I kissed him on the cheek.

We were sitting across from each other, our eyes locked and our hearts as well. "I wanted you to have this because you are my star. You are the star of my night and my days."

"It is so beautiful." I couldn't do anything but repeat myself; no other words were worthy of the task.

"I don't need to look at the sky; my star is sitting right across from me now."

I put the necklace on, hoping it would be tight enough to cut off the flow of tears.

He rubbed his hands together. "And now?"

He was expecting a present, but I didn't have one. I looked at books, CDs, and videos, but they just seemed wrong. I guess I was more afraid of upsetting him by getting him the wrong thing than I was excited about getting him the right thing.

"Paul, I don't really have anything; I'm sorry." I was so ashamed. "The only gift I would like to give you is my heart, but you already have that."

"You could come to Stanford with me next fall," he said, stumbling over the words.

"Paul, please." I closed my eyes and touched the necklace.

"I know, but it was worth a shot." Paul smiled, but I knew he was faking it.

"Let me give you this," I said, "Turn over; let me rub your back."

"Well, you are, as Brad used to say, the Chief," he said, and then rolled over.

As my skin merged with his in the dim light in this room, it all came together for me. Just under a year ago, I was this shy girl who took a risk and asked this quirky senior guy to kiss me because he was all I wanted. Now I was the one about to be a senior, and things had changed. He was asking me, not for a kiss, but for something more. This time I was the one saying no.

"Paul, can I ask you something?" I whispered.

"On or off the record?" he replied. "Are you taping this? And if so, where could you possibly be hiding a tape recorder? I think I've done a full-body search."

"Paul, do you love me?" I asked, hesitating with each word.

"What a silly question." He started to turn around, but I kept my hands pressed against him. I didn't want him to see me wearing his beautiful gift while thinking these ugly thoughts.

I took a deep breath. "Do you love me, Paul?" I asked again.

I couldn't keep him down; he turned to face me. "Of course I do."

"Then why don't you ever tell me that?" Paul only told me he loved me after he hurt me.

"You know I do." He put his hands on my face, then moved his fingers slowly down my shoulder, then down my arms, passing over the bruises on both.

I collapsed onto him. I needed to hear those words. I needed to capture the memory of my head resting on his chest, the hairs tickling my nose. I took in the smell, the sound, the touch; I locked it all in.

"My turn," he said.

"I love you, Paul." Without hesitation I said it and felt it and lived it.

"I know you hated me last winter. I don't blame you." Each word sounded like a confession. "I never meant to hurt you. I'm sorry about the stuff that happened between us."

"That's behind us," I said, trying to convince myself. I knew it was far from behind us. Lying there naked, the evidence was right in front of us on my bruised arms. There had not been a repeat of his savage attack on me, like the one the night of the Valentine's dance, but the pushing, pulling, jabbing, and even name-calling continued. My long sleeves covered the bruises, my excuses hid the truth, and my fear of my heart breaking again stopped us from breaking up.

"Joha, do you forgive me?" he asked.

"Of course." Again, I responded without hesitation. "Now it is my turn again."

"What are you talking about?" he said, stroking my hair.

"Paul, will you forgive me?" I asked in a whisper.

"Joha, you haven't done anything," he said just as softly.

"Just tell me that you forgive me." I was speaking directly into his chest, my words pushing through skin, muscle, and bone to speak directly to his heart. "Now, when we're happy, just tell me that you'll forgive me."

Paul moved down in the bed, so that we were face to face. He brushed the hair out of my tear-filled eyes, which defied and defined me; I wanted and needed to be strong.

"I will never hurt you again, Joha." He kissed me, long and soft and tender.

It was so easy for him to say these words, so hard for him to act upon them. Paul was sorry for how he acted, but he wasn't sorry for who he was. "Say what I want to hear," I begged.

"Joha, don't cry." He tried kissing away the tears, but there were too many.

I pressed up so close to him that I couldn't even see him. "Tell me, tell me!"

"Of course I'll forgive you, but I know you will never hurt me, Joha." He rolled us over, taking us right to the very edge of the bed. We were seconds away from crashing. He kissed me, then whispered into my ear, "You will *never* hurt me."

We looked at each other for a long while, our throats and

hearts exhausted. After a while Paul got up and moved toward the shower. "Climb in?" he asked, as I watched him disappear into the bathroom.

"Give me a minute, okay?" I replied. When I heard the water start, I got up and quickly moved over to the desk. I found a pen and some of the hotel stationery. I wiped away the last few tears, making sure not to stain the paper. And I started writing.

"Dear Paul,"

THIRTY

"Hey, good luck tomorrow," Lynne said. Kara and Jackie nodded in agreement.

With school starting tomorrow, the four of us were enjoying one last mall fast-food-court dinner break together. I had decided to quit my job at the bookstore and concentrate on school, which was starting tomorrow. Getting lousy grades might spite my parents, but it accomplished little else. I had to get my priorities straight.

"We've got to find you something outrageous to wear for the first day of your senior year," Kara said. "Two months of hanging out with us and you still don't know how to dress!"

"I know, I know." I said with a laugh. I still didn't have the knack; but then again, wearing long sleeves twenty-four/seven would make anyone look like a fashion idiot.

"Let's blow your last check and my employee discount in one swell foop!" Kara said, trying to sound happy, but we all knew she was still hurting from Brad leaving.

"Maybe you should spend some money on clothes for Paul," Lynne said with a grin.

"Why's that?" I asked.

"I think Paul's been wearing the same outfit of jeans, T-shirts, and black high-tops as long as we've known him," Lynne said, while Jackie fought back a smirk.

"He's one of a kind," I said, adding a sigh for comic effect.

"Not really. I had an ex like that," Jackie said. "You guys remember Dave Hitchings?"

"I'd rather not," Kara said.

"Who was that?" I asked. While I was tight with Kara, I still wasn't in the inner circle. I'd yet to gain access to the sharing of ex-boyfriend stories, secrets, and sex histories.

"This older guy I went out with. I was in ninth grade, and he was a senior," Jackie said, slightly struggling with her words. "When I met him, he already had a girlfriend; but I was young and stupid and all flattered that he paid attention to me. So he cheated on her with me, then finally dumped her, and I was so happy."

"What happened?" I asked.

"What do you think happened, Johanna?" Jackie replied sharply. "Within a couple of months, he was cheating on me with somebody else."

"What a dickhead," Kara said. Lynne nodded in instant agreement.

"It is the worst feeling in the world being lied to like that," Jackie said, but then let out a small, almost sad laugh. "But I should have known, right? When I met him, he was going out with someone else. I should have known if he would cheat on another girl, he would do the same to me. I didn't see. I didn't want to see it."

"I'm so sorry." I handed her a napkin to wipe away those angry tears. I wanted to hug her, hold her, and take all the hurt away. Maybe by letting her share it, I was doing that.

"Don't be so sorry for me. I knew better. That's the worst part." Jackie wrapped her hands around her coffee cup.

"You were being lied to; how could you know," I said, then noticed that Kara was staring right at me.

"How could I know?" Jackie just shook her head. "Because he did it before. I guess some people change, but I bet he never did. He's probably telling the same lies to some other girl that he told to me."

"None of us really get lied to; we mostly just lie to ourselves," Kara said, but I noticed that again, she was looking right at me, not at Jackie.

"I guess that's the kind of stuff I wish I would have learned in school rather than the hard way," Jackie said as she finished up her coffee.

"I wonder what that son of a bitch is up to now?" Lynne asked.

"The same thing, I just know it," Jackie said, her voice caught between laughter and tears. "I bet you to this day Dave Hitchings is still cheating on his girlfriends, telling them the same stories of how he'll change."

"If they did it before, they'll do it again," Kara said, once again her eyes fixed on me.

As Lynne, Jackie, and Kara chatted on, I slumped into my seat. They kept talking, but I wasn't hearing anything; instead, I was gently rubbing my hand over the most recent bruise on my arm and heard Kara's words ring in my head: "If they did it before, they'll do it again."

After Lynne and Jackie headed back to work, Kara and I headed to the clothing store. Once inside, Kara moved from rack to rack like a whirling dervish. "This is it!"

"I don't think so," I said, looking at the way too small, way too revealing dress.

"Come back here with me, and let's try it on." She walked to the dressing rooms in the back of the store and held the door open for me, her foot tapping impatiently.

"It is not that, but—" I started.

"Don't you like the dress?" Kara asked. "Don't be afraid to show skin, kid."

"The dress is fine," I said, then started to cry.

"What's wrong?" Kara took a step toward me.

I didn't answer. I stood there with my head down, wanting the carpet to swallow me.

"Johanna, talk to me. Tell me what's wrong," Kara said. But I wasn't listening to her; instead, I was remembering something she had told me last spring: "If you want to be saved, you need to reach out," and hearing her words from earlier: "If they did it before, they'll do it again."

I walked inside the dressing room and shut the door behind me. I unbuttoned my shirt and let it fall to the floor as Kara gasped.

"Did Paul do this?" Kara's words bounced around the small confines of the dressing room. I stood there looking at the floor, my bruised arms exposed for her to examine.

"Sometimes he gets angry at me or frustrated with his world. He promised when we got back together that it wouldn't happen again, but it didn't last. He misses Brad, he hates when I spend time with you, he hates his job, and he hates that I have a job and I don't see him as much. He's angry and blames me. He pushes, he grabs, he squeezes." I was speaking softly. The people next to us didn't need to know this, even if I finally needed to tell it.

"No, no." Kara was shaking her head back and forth. She was mad at Paul, but I sensed she was even angrier with me, and I can't say that I blamed her. "Why didn't you tell someone?"

"I don't know," I said, holding back tears. "I was ashamed, afraid. I just couldn't."

"Not even your parents?" Kara asked.

"Especially not them," I replied. "I can't let them know they were right about Paul."

"What about someone at school? What about Mr. Taylor or one of the counselors?"

"No, I couldn't tell anyone that someone who supposed to be smart is really so dumb."

"How could you let him do this?" Kara asked gently.

"He is so gentle most times, his touch so soft." I felt tears coming, pushing my words faster now. "But other times, he'll grab me so hard, it leaves a mark like this. Or sometimes he'll push me against something."

"Leave him, now," Kara said, the words clipped. "Damn you, leave him, now."

"I tried, but I can't; I just can't do it. You know what that is like." I sat down on the small bench; Kara sat down next to me, putting her arms around me. Paul called me star, but he was my sun. I couldn't break free of his pull. "Kara, as bad as this hurts, leaving him would be worse. When we broke up last winter, I thought I was going to die."

I told her the whole story about the night of the Valentine's Day dance, sparing no details. I told her how I tried to run away, but couldn't.

"You got back in the car with him?" Kara was growing angrier with each revelation.

"What else could I do?" I asked her. "If not, he would have just hit me again. If I ran away, it would just be the same scene over and over again."

Kara hugged me hard, her thumbs pressing softly against Paul's latest anger tattoo. "Do you hear yourself?"

"What?"

Kara let go of my arms and tapped on the mirror. "Stand up and look at yourself."

I did as she said. I stared at my pitiful image in the mirror and hated it.

"I know, I know." I just shook my head.

"If you don't run away, then it will play over and over again; you have to know that!"

I was on automatic pilot. "I know, I know."

"Put this on." I took the dress from her hands, dropped my jeans, and put the dress on. She'd sized me up. As she zipped it in back I could tell the dress was almost a perfect fit.

"You look beautiful," Kara said, now standing next to me.

"You lie," I said.

"Johanna, what are you going to do?" she whispered.

"I know what I need to do, but I can't. It's too hard. I love him so much."

"Johanna, you have to do something," Kara pressed on.

"You don't understand. I don't even understand." My eyes were closed.

"You might as well take that dress off, then," Kara said, reaching over to undo the zipper.

"But you said it looked good!" I protested as the dress fell down around my knees.

Kara sighed. "You don't need that dress. Unless you do the hard thing, picking out clothes will be easy. It looks like you plan on wearing long sleeves the rest of your life."

"No, this is just a bad time. I know things will change. Things will get better," I told her, unsure if I believed those lies anymore.

Kara took a deep breath. She started to speak, but each time she would suck back her words.

"Kara, what's wrong?" I asked.

"I suspected," Kara said. She was near tears now. "I need to tell you something."

"What?"

"God, I should have told you this a long time ago," Kara continued. "But I couldn't. I couldn't hurt Brad; you know that, don't you?"

"What are you talking about?"

"Last year, the prom. I told you that we went with Carla and Paul. I need to tell you about Carla."

"What about her?" I was almost begging.

"I saw her the next day. I told Brad about it, but he said I couldn't say anything to you. He wanted to protect Paul. I guess someone should have protected you from him."

"Kara, what are you trying to say."

"The day after the prom. The four of us were supposed to get together, but Carla never showed. I wondered what was going on, so I went over to her house."

"And?"

"When she came down to answer the door, that's when I saw it," Kara continued.

"Saw what?"

"Carla had a black eye," Kara said. The sound of my pulse was shattering my eardrums.

I ran my hand over my arm, feeling the bruises.

"I wanted to tell you, but I couldn't betray Brad. I promised him I wouldn't tell you. He said he was for Paul, right or wrong. He said it would be the end of us if I told. And I knew you were smart. I thought you would know what do to," Kara said, her voice choked with emotion.

"A black eye," I repeated, and I remembered looking in the mirror that night after the Valentine's Day dance.

"I'm so sorry," Kara said.

I couldn't speak. I couldn't move.

"I should have told you. I'm so sorry," Kara repeated. "What are you going to do?"

"I guess it is like Mr. Taylor told me once. There are two sides to every story," I said after a long silence. "I heard Paul's side; maybe I need to hear Carla's."

"Use this," Kara said as she handed me her cell phone and left me alone in the changing room. "Her name is Carla Stevenson, and she lives on Long Lake Road."

I put my glasses back on and took one long last look in the mirror at my bruised arms. This image reflecting back at me wasn't just a picture of my past, and it wasn't just a mirror of my present; it was also a crystal ball of my future.

It was easy to do.

It took just one phone call.

Carla was still at home; she wasn't going back to college until after Labor Day. She denied it at first, just like I had. But I pressed her, using every journalistic skill in my bag. Using years of lessons on interrogation I had learned by osmosis from my mother. It took a while, but I got her side of the story. I got the story of how Paul would hit her. How he would drink, get angry, and then hit her. Grab her too tight; push her against things. Sometimes, she said, he did it when he didn't drink; she never knew what set him off. She never told anyone, she said. Like me, she lied about her bruises or hid them under layers of clothing. Carla told me of his promises to change, over and over again. That was Carla's story; it was my story, too.

By the time I was off the phone, it was almost nine o'clock. I ran from the mall and jumped into my mom's Jeep. I almost drove the car off the road as I raced over to Wallie's parking lot. I would wait there until Paul got off at eleven, then confront him. I was just pulling in when I saw Paul get in the Firebird, leaving work two hours early. Damn him.

He drove so fast that it was hard to follow him. I was just about to give up and decide to meet him at his trailer when I saw him turn off an exit too soon.

I followed him, my hands shaking on the wheel, my eyes so full with tears and my heart so full of hate that I don't know how I stayed on the road.

I followed him, watching as he turned the car into the parking lot of the Atlas Mini-Storage, off Telegraph Road. What in bloody hell was he doing here at this hour?

I drove past, letting him turn in. I did a U-turn and parked across the street at the Pizza Hut. Outside, I heard the noise of people laughing, out on dates, falling in love.

They were falling in love, but I was just falling. And now I was waiting. Waiting and wanting.

I waited almost two hours until I saw the headlights of the Firebird come out from behind the security gate. I gunned the engine, my hands shaking like they had fallen on a live wire. I drove across the road and put my car about five feet in front of his in the parking lot of the Atlas Mini-Storage. He was trapped. He wasn't going anywhere.

I jumped out of the car and marched over to the passenger side of the Firebird. Like a hundred times before, in one smooth move, Paul opened the door for me with his foot while pushing a CD into the player with his hand. He had no idea what he had just let into his car as the sounds of "Thunder Road" filled that small space we had shared so many times.

"Star, what are you—"

"I hate you!" I screamed at him; even through the tears, I made the words clear.

"Joha, what is the—"

"You bastard! You lied to me! I hate you!" My fists were clinched so tight, I thought I was going to pinch my fingers off.

"Calm down, calm down, just calm down." He was repeating himself. He was slurring his words. He was drunk.

"You lied to me! You bastard!" I couldn't stop shaking even once I sat down.

"What are you talking about?" Paul said as I reached over to eject the CD, but he grabbed my hand.

"Don't you touch me!" I shouted at him and pulled my hand away. I pulled my arms around me; I was so cold, so very cold.

"What's wrong, Star?" His eyes showed his confusion, his lack of sobriety, and his lie.

"I'll tell you what is wrong." I was rocking back and forth, trying to somehow push some of the pain away. "But I have to ask you a question first."

"What?" His tone was catching up with mine; he snapped off the words.

"Did you make love to Carla before or after you beat her up?" I was a crazy woman; I was a wild woman. I didn't care.

"What are you talking about?" The panic in his voice was so obvious. I knew, and I could tell that he knew that I knew.

"You know what I am talking about," I said, staring him down. "You lied to me."

"I don't know what you are—"

"Don't you dare! Don't you dare sit here and lie to me any-more!" I was enraged. "Listen to me; I know. I know about you and Carla!"

"Is that some crap that idiot Kara told you?"

"Do you want to know how I know?" I asked, never giving him a chance to answer. "I talked to her. God, why didn't I do that months ago?"

"You did what?"

"I talked to Carla. She told me how you hit her. How you slapped her. Bruised her arms and blackened her eyes. How you beat her up after the prom. She told me how you said you would change. I knew her story, Paul. I knew every word because it happened to me, too!"

"Listen, that was just the one time." He was pushing himself against the door, as far from me as possible in the cage the Firebird had turned into.

"How can you sit there and lie to me?" I screeched at him.

"You never asked me, so I never lied."

"More lies. I asked you if you had ever hurt anyone like you hurt me, and you told me no." My damn memory. Despite being filled with formulas and proofs, I had allowed lots of room in my brain for Paul. He had a whole wing. I filed every word. I remembered the conversations, the questions and answers, and so did he. He was lying to me still.

"Get out of my car," Paul said in a voice that sounded almost dead.

"What are you doing here?" I asked. I had been sitting in the parking lot of Pizza Hut trying to get my mind around it. What was he doing at a mini-storage facility at eleven at night?

"None of your damn business." He jabbed his index finger at me, hard into my shoulder. I could feel the bruise forming. My body's memory knew that process all too well.

"More secrets. What other things are you hiding from me?" I asked.

"I said, it is none of your—"

"This is so you, Paul. I've been such an idiot." I slapped my forehead with my palm, trying to knock some sense into my head. "You hide things. Is this where you drink?"

The dome light of the car was off, the lights of the parking lot dim; but I could see those green eyes glaring at me, cutting through me. He turned the music up, trying to drown me out. Springsteen's "Back Streets" filled the car, but I was shouting louder than Bruce could sing.

"You promised me. Promised me you would change. I saw you dump the beer out that day I told you I was getting a job. You promised me you wouldn't drink anymore. You lied."

More angry silence from Paul; more impassioned vocals from Bruce.

"You try to hide it. Like you are hiding whatever you do here."

He sprang at me. He grabbed my arm and twisted it. "I'm not hiding. I'm right here for you to see! That is, whenever you find the time for me. I wanted to leave Pontiac, but I stayed here because of you. Now you give me this shit!"

"You stayed for you, not for me. You stayed because you were afraid to leave."

"The truth is I should be at Stanford right now," he shouted.

"No, the truth is what Carla told me. I keep forgiving you, Paul; I keep forgiving you, thinking that you will change. But you don't. You don't even try."

"Shut up!" He shouted at me, and then tried to wrap his hand around my mouth.

I pushed him away. "I can't believe I let you touch me. You beat Carla up, and you beat me up. Why do you act this way?"

"Sometimes I get angry, that's all." He wasn't looking at me.

"So do I, Paul; but I don't hurt people like you. It's not that simple." He had the air-conditioning in the car turned up, and I was starting to shiver. My muscles were remembering that February night; my eyes were reliving Paul kicking the Dumpster, then hitting me. "You hurt people. I've seen you put people down with your tongue. I heard you call me names. I know how you talk to your mother. I know how you lied about Pam. I hear the names you call Kara. And now I know what you did to Carla. I know how you hurt me and hurt yourself."

"No, that's not true, Joha; you have to understand—"

"And now, you're drunk." I moved closer to catch the aroma. "I can smell it."

"Just give me a chance, Joha, just a chance." He hands moved toward me, like so many times before in this small space; but I retreated back into the corner.

"I gave you a chance after you pulled that stunt at Santi's. I gave you a chance when you lied to me about why you didn't go away to school. I gave you a chance after you hit me in February. I gave you chance after chance after you bruised me, thinking if I didn't say anything, it would stop. Thinking it was my fault and that I couldn't live without you. You've run out of chances."

"Don't say that," Paul said softly. "One more chance; this time it will be different."

"You don't want another chance, you want twenty more." In the darkness of this godforsaken mini-storage parking lot, everything was coming to light. "Paul, I don't believe you. You told Carla you would stop, and you didn't. You told me you would stop, and you didn't. I can't give you any more chances. I don't want to wear long sleeves the rest of my life."

"Shut up!" Paul, realizing soft wasn't working, returned to hard words delivered harshly.

This was it. This was our final exam. I moved over, my face almost on top of his. I took off my glasses and set them on the dash so I could get as close as possible. "You want to hit me now, don't you?"

"You shut the fuck up!" He shouted at me, his mouth almost bumping against my ear.

"Go ahead, Paul. It doesn't matter now. Nothing matters to me now." I was as crazed as he was, maybe more so.

"I said shut up!" I watched his right hand, expecting it, like the times before, to sweep in high, but he surprised me. Both hands came from below, like a cobra, and wrapped around my throat. "Shut up! Shut up! SHUT UP!!!!!!!!!"

He was screaming into my ear and choking me. I tried to pull his hands away from me, but he had strength and he had leverage that even in all my fury, I couldn't match. I was coughing, trying to scream, but he was strangling the words in my throat.

I managed to get his right hand from around my throat, breaking my star necklace in the process; but that was a mistake. His right hand now free, he raised it high in the air, formed a fist, and brought it down hard against my face, over my left eye. I tried to scream in pain; but with his left hand still around my throat, I could only push two words through, "Please, Paul."

He stared back at me, then took his hands off my throat and slammed them time and time again into the dashboard until blood was spurting from the cuts on the sides of his hands.

I sat back, breathing in deeply, holding my head and feeling the blood trickle down my face. Paul sat forward, his head resting on the steering wheel, his bloody hands pushed against his face. The ordeal had sucked all the tears from my body and the energy from both of us. Trapped in the small space, we said nothing as Springsteen sang about being "Born to Run." Part of me wanted to reach over and touch him, just run my fingers through the long blond hair like I had so many times before. Part of me believed I could make him feel better, take that pain away. That part of me was dying.

"Why do you hate me?" Paul asked, his voice as lonesome as I could imagine.

It took all the energy I had to resist hugging him; he knew me too well; he knew what I would do; he knew how to get the reaction he wanted out of me. "I don't hate you, but I can't go on like this. I hate that you lied to me, and I hate what you did to me and to Carla."

"You do hate me." He sounded as if he was going to cry. "You don't care about me."

"I loved you, Paul." I made sure to use the past tense. "I loved you so much."

"They why are you leaving me here?" Paul did this often, and it had always worked. He made me feel sorry for him. He burrowed his head into my shoulders.

"Paul, I just—" I put on my glasses and resisted the temptation to comfort him.

"Don't leave me! Oh, God, please Johanna, please don't leave me." I could barely understand his words; they were wrapped in tears.

This was it. This was what I knew I would have to say. I just didn't know it would be so soon, although I figured it would be taking place in the Firebird, my second home. "I've never lived anywhere else. I've never loved anyone else. I've never made love to anyone else."

"Why are you saying this?" He put his hand on the seat next to me; the blood was flowing into the upholstery. "You don't want to be with me anymore, so what does it matter."

I took a deep breath. I needed all the power I had in my lungs and heart. "I know, Paul, it's over."

We were not breaking up; we were breaking down.

"Listen, about Carla, let me explain." He tried brushing his hand against the side of my face, but I moved his hand away.

"There is no explanation, Paul. That's what you're not hearing. I'm sure you have reasons and excuses, but none of them matter. You don't hit other people; you don't beat up and bruise people that you say you love."

"Don't say it like that; it was once or twice." He said it like he was twelve years old, trying to make excuses for taking too many cookies. "I won't do it again, Johanna, I swear."

"Paul, I talked to Carla. It wasn't once or twice; it was more. It was a lot."

"Look, I was having a bad time then, maybe drinking too much, but—"

"No, Paul, that's not the truth." I was done shouting; my throat was dry and sore from the screaming on the inside, the choking on the outside.

"I know I won't. I promise I'll change." He put his hands together, like he was praying. "I'll quit drinking; everything is going to be okay. Joha, please, please trust me."

"Paul, everything is not going to be okay." I turned back the words that used to be so soothing to me; now the same words were just smothering. "I don't trust you."

"Johanna, please, I won't drink anymore. I won't do it again. I won't—"

"Paul, you broke that promise already." I pointed to the swelling around my left eye. "It's not the drinking, Paul. It's you. It's you, Paul."

"No, this time, Joha, Star, this time—"

"There is no this time or next time. We are over." I couldn't believe I said the words.

He grabbed me by the shoulders. I didn't resist. I could tell he didn't know what to do or say. I guessed part of him wanted to hold me; the other half wanted to hit me. In the darkness of this deserted parking lot, I was seeing those two sides of Paul battling right before my eyes.

"No, Star, please don't say that; everything is going to be different." His forehead was against mine; he was speaking softly, slowly. It was like we were in bed, pressed up against each other, like nothing else in the world mattered.

"Paul, please, listen to me." He looked at me, those green eyes sparkling with tears, loaded with fears. "You say that; you say everything is going to be different; but it never is. When I learned what happened to Carla, I knew it wasn't just me, and that is what scares me worst of all. If I stayed with you, this would just keep happening again and again."

"No, this time, really, Joha—" he touched my hands, but I felt nothing.

"It's not just because you hit me. It's not because you lied to me. It's not because you keep drinking. It is because you can't stop doing these things, and that scares me to death."

Sitting in my seat, digging my short, well-chewed fingernails into the beaten-down black upholstery, I looked down at the cluttered floor thinking about what I had yet to say: the words that would break my heart, but probably save my life.

"One more chance, Joha, just one more chance, please," Paul begged.

"Paul, you are part of my past, not part of my future." I ended it.

He slumped back in his seat. I never looked up as I opened the door of the Firebird. I knew in about a year I would start college at Columbia. After I graduated from there, I hoped I could see the world, write stories for newspapers or magazines, and visit every corner of the globe. But I wondered if I might ever travel again any greater distance than the distance between the Firebird and my mother's Jeep.

After I got back into my car, I sat there, watching as Paul quickly backed up. He pulled around me, leaving a patch in the parking lot of the Atlas Mini-Storage. I tried not to watch the tail-lights of the Firebird, but the temptation was too great, the habit too strong. So many times I had watched him Firebirding down the road after a morning, a day, or an evening we spent together, making me laugh or smile; watched him Firebirding down the road after bringing me ice cream or roses; Firebirding down the road after spending the time in a crowded movie theater on a Saturday night. But as I watched those taillights disappear in front of me on this cool Michigan September night I knew in every fiber of my body that it was for the last time. I didn't need to taste any tears to know my life was mine and that it would never be the same again.

THIRTY-TWO

Dear Dead Dad:
It lasted from the first "I want you to kiss me" to
the last "you are part of my past, not part of my future," and now it was over. Over. Dead, just like
you. I have not slept for almost twenty-four hours. I
drove all night; but even still, no matter how many
miles I covered, I couldn't deal with the distance.

It wasn't the distance on the road. It wasn't the
distance that was now and forever between Johanna
and me. It wasn't the distance between the steering
wheel and the gas pedal; between the gas pedal and
the wheels; between the wheels and the road. It
wasn't the distance between what was and what would
never be again. It wasn't the distance between her
tears and my fears. It wasn't even the distance
between the truth and the lie: between the part of
me that wants to die *("it's a suicide rap")*, and the
part of me that wants to live.

Dad, it is the distance between innocence and
experience.

Dad, it is the distance between the womb and the
world.

Is that what scared you?

I finally have you figured out, dead man. I know
why you drank and why you hit Mom and why you ran
away. You were afraid. I don't know what you were
afraid of other than life itself, which can be
pretty damn scary I have to admit; but I won't let
it get to me.

I know you; I know everything about you. I listen
to your music and I live your life, but I will be
better than you. I will change, and Johanna will
take me back. You hang your hoods in hell, dead man,
but I'll be out of this town full of losers before
you know it.

There was an envelope on the table when I
finally came home the next morning. Mom said that
Johanna had dropped it off and that she looked terrible. When I came home, Mom didn't comment on my
appearance; it was obvious. She said she was sorry,
and she didn't mention Jesus even once. I picked up
the envelope. I had been through this before. But
this time it was light. Ashes. That is all I
thought it was. She took everything and burned it.
Turned them, like us, into ashes. Burning hot, but
utterly useless.

I opened it, dreading what was inside. I poured
out the contents; but there were not ashes, there
was just a note. This note did not tell the twelve-
year-old me to tell my mother that her husband and
my father was running away from his responsibility.
This note did not reassure me that everything would

be okay as I watched our bills mount, watched my mother turn to Jesus, and watched our house get turned into a trailer and me into a trash bag. This note did not say "trust me," because that is just another lie.

Guess what, Dad? Everything was not, and is not, okay.

Instead, there was a note from Johanna. It was written on stationery from the Hilton, from our night together in August.

Dear Paul,

I am writing this as you are in the shower. We knew this day would come. I don't know, sitting in this hotel room, what either of us is feeling as you are reading this.

I don't want you to hate me.

If I told you that I hated you, I didn't mean it.

If we are breaking up, then I want us to promise to hold on to all of the good memories we have created for each other.

I want us, once some time has passed, to be able to forgive each other and maybe even become friends. There is not much I can write that you don't already know, but if you don't mind me saying it again, I think you are wonderful, the best thing that ever happened to me. I love you more than I could ever tell you or show you. Despite the bravado you might have observed that first day in your car when I asked you to kiss me, I was really a mess. You cleaned me up. You made me a better person. You made me laugh, and you loved me. I hope you will remember me. I know I will remember you.

As I told you just moments ago as we lay together on the bed, no matter what, we need to forgive each other. We've meant too much to each other for too long to have anything but love between us. I wouldn't trade my memories of you for anything in the world. I will keep them, my thoughts of you and this beautiful star-shaped necklace that you gave me tonight, forever. You are my first love, and you will last forever. I don't know why you are reading this other than we must have decided to break up. Paul, I know we will break up; but we will never be broken. What we had will last forever. We will always be together.

I want you to miss me because I know that I will miss you.

Love,
Johanna aka Joha aka Star

The screen door slammed. I stepped out on the porch wearing a white sleeveless dress my parents had bought me for this graduation party. I watched as Paul pushed his blond hair out of his eyes as he slowed the car down and pulled into the driveway. He must have turned the volume up on the CD player to push the loud crashing sounds of Springsteen's "Thunder Road" through the open windows and out into the warm Michigan June twilight.

It would be my first time seeing Paul since that night nine months ago, just before my senior year started. I had avoided both going to Santi's and looking for black Firebirds. I had also avoided talking with my parents about the breakup. They had been right about Paul in some ways, but I could never let them know, at least not yet. Things were tense in our house through fall and winter, as my mother and I had silently agreed not to speak to each other. It wasn't stupid, like refusing to ask her to pass the salt at dinner, but my mother and I became strangers. But lately, we are starting to have conversations again rather than playing twenty questions. My hope, my brightest desperate hope, is that we will become friends somehow, someday. Maybe it will be when we both stop expecting me to be perfect. My experience with Paul certainly taught me that I was far from perfect and that in lots of things, like matters of the heart, being smart really doesn't help all that much.

"Paul, you're really here," I hugged him immediately as we met in the driveway.

"Thanks for the invite," he said, looking like he was trying to hold back his usual smirk.

"I'm so glad you made it." I said it and I meant it. I had gone back and forth, back and forth, about inviting him to my celebration of high school ending. I was going to Columbia University in New York to study journalism in the fall, not the University of Michigan to become an engineer like my father. My parents were disappointed in my choice, but they tried not to show it or be angry about it. They were learning to let go; now I needed to do the same.

Kara, Lynne, and Jackie and their dates all arrived early and stayed late. Mr. Taylor and Mr. Edwards were both there, and so were Pam and Dylan. While Pam and I never really became close friends again, it was important she showed. She and Dylan were in love, and both were going to school at Michigan State. Brad couldn't make it to the party; he was staying in California over the summer, but he sent a card and the book *Zen and the Art of Motorcycle Maintenance*.

Everyone that mattered to me in high school was there, so Paul had to come. He was part of it, a good part for some time. I had loved him. Or thought I did. I still don't know, and I wonder sometimes if I ever will really know.

"I really can't stay," Paul said. He kicked his ankles together and pushed his hair back. It was as long as ever.

"That's too bad," I said sadly, looking past Paul out toward the Firebird. He was not alone. I knew better, but for a second I was jealous. "Doesn't your friend want to come in?"

Paul glanced back at the Firebird. The engine running, the

music blaring. It now sounded like "She's the One." I hadn't listened to Springsteen for over eight months, so the songs were no longer burned in my brain like a personal party mix CD.

"No, we can only stay for a minute," he said.

Maybe this was my first test as an adult. "I'd like to meet her, really. I'd like to meet—"

"Sarah. She's a junior over at South High. I met her at work over at Wallie's. She's a hostess, and her dad is one of my managers," Paul said, his smile bright as ever.

I looked at the girl sitting in the Firebird with the multicolored hair wearing very dark sunglasses even in the twilight of the evening. "I'd really like to meet her."

Paul didn't move. "There is something I need to do first," Paul said. He nervously reached into the front pocket of his torn blue jeans and pulled out a small black box.

I looked quickly at the girl in the Firebird, then glanced at the box. "You really didn't—"

With a sense of urgency, Paul handed me the box. "Open it."

I looked inside. There was my silver star-shaped necklace. "Paul, this is—"

"That night, you know, in the car it got—" Paul said slowly. "It fell off by accident."

I took the necklace out. I didn't know what to say or do as Paul slipped his arms around my neck. He pushed my now short hair up as he fastened the clasp. Instinct washed over me. I turned to face Paul, then held him tightly. He turned his face away, resting his head on my shoulder, holding me tight. I didn't care if Marcus saw it; I would explain it to him later. He would understand; he had been a great boyfriend since we got together a few months ago. I will miss him when I go away to school in the fall.

As Paul held me, muscle memories, like dancing at the prom, like lying in bed together, all our good times, tugged at me. How had I been strong enough to pull away from this?

"Look, I really gotta go," Paul said, pulling away from me. "Sarah is waiting."

"I really would like to meet her."

As we walked toward the Firebird there was nothing but silence between us. At the car, Paul opened the door.

"Johanna, this is Sarah," Paul said.

Even with her eyes hidden behind sunglasses, she didn't try to make contact.

"Nice to meet you," Sarah said to me almost in a monotone. "Paul, we're late for that other party. Can we go?"

"Look, we really gotta hit the road," Paul said as he moved toward the other side of the Firebird.

As my eyes followed Paul I noticed he seemed to be keeping one hand on the hood of the car as if to keep his balance. My eyes quickly darted to the backseat; there was a pile of empty Stroh's beer cans. As the Firebird started to back out, I noticed that Sarah was taking off her sunglasses. Even from a distance I noticed Sarah's stunning green eyes, especially the one blackened by the back of Paul's hand.

The following is an excerpt of a conversation between Patrick Jones and the tenth-grade students in Kim Powers and Laura Gajdostik's Young Adult Literature class at Hudson High School, Wisconsin, on his novel Things Change.

To read the interview in its entirety, visit
www.connectingya.com/thingschange
or
www.walkeryoungreaders.com

How did you think of the title of the book?
I always knew the "punch line" of the book: that Paul would not change. Given that, I wanted an ironic title. But more than that, what two-word expression could better define the world that teens live in than one where everything changes. Also, the title fits since just about everything except the first and last line did change as I rewrote the book.

What inspired you to write about a couple of teenagers?
Most of my work in libraries has been directly related to teens, from being a young-adult librarian to now working with teens in correctional facilities. Because of that, about the only fiction I read is young-adult literature. I find teens fascinating on so many levels. Here are these people, often treated by their parents or other adults as children, who obviously engage in adult activities. The conflicts of the teen years are so huge that I don't understand how anyone would not want to write about teens, and I can't imagine writing a book for adults.

Do you think teenagers can experience "love" or do they just think they are?

Of everything that Bruce Springsteen has written, these are the key lines from one of his all-time best songs, "Born to Run." He sings, "I want to know if love is wild. I want to know if love is real." I think both Paul and Johanna are asking themselves that same question: is this love real? Yes, teens do feel love, differently than adults, but an emotion so raw, so real, and for Johanna in particular, so overwhelming. Her heart rules her head, and that's really the central conflict in the novel. Yet, that love has consequences and it doesn't solve all of her problems; instead it creates a new set of issues for her. I think Paul in his own broken way does love Johanna, but can't get it right. I think every book I write for teens is going to be about passion, romance, sex, love—whatever you want to call it—because for teens it is all new, exciting, and consuming.

Where did you get all the ideas about dating and its controversies?

I was visiting a high school one day and saw this girl backed up against her locker. She had in her hands lots of big, thick textbooks, like Chemistry and Trig. A boy—I assume her boyfriend but couldn't know—was leaning against her, talking right into her face. I could tell she wanted to leave, but he was certainly bigger, probably stronger, and she was trapped. So the question I asked is one that all writers ask when they see something: how come? How did this smart girl get herself in this situation? She had to know better, so why was she letting herself be pushed around? After the book was almost done, I finally did some research about teen dating violence and found that I'd gotten almost every detail, every sign and symptom, right on for both Paul and Johanna. That scene later worked its way into the book directly—although Vickie was the girl pushed up against the locker, not Johanna.

Is it hard to make a character, such as Paul, so nice at times and so mean at others?

That's important to the story: if he's just an asshole, then people would think Johanna was stupid for falling in love with him. Readers—who more than likely are teenage girls themselves—have to find Paul likable, so they can understand why Johanna loves him and stays with him. Paul also needs to show both faces to Johanna: when he hurts her, he apologizes, buys her gifts, and is nice again. Sadly, that's the pattern of abuse. Also, most everyone has their good sides and bad. It's just that for Paul, the gulf between the two is huge. He's not a monster, but he does monstrous things. I think all teens have two sides—heck, look at Johanna, honor student by day, "visiting the grandparents by night"—but in Paul those two sides are intense. I think the cover of the book captures the two sides of Paul: those red drops are BOTH rose petals and blood drops.

Can you relate to Paul's life in any way?

Let's just say this: Paul is the worst version of myself at that age. One of my former high school teachers uses *Things Change* with her classes and recognizes me in some aspects of the Paul character. I did drive a black Firebird, for instance. I didn't listen to Springsteen however, being more into the Rolling Stones my junior year (*Some Girls*), the Who (*The Kids Are Alright*), and the beginnings of punk and new wave. So Paul's obsession with music is very familiar to me, even if the soundtrack is different. *Nailed* [my next novel] is much, much more like my high school years, and that's not necessarily a good thing for the main character! Oh, and I did wear tennis shoes to my prom.

Do you feel that this book helps change teens' perspectives on their lives?

A lot of people think if you write for teens that you owe it to them to teach a lesson, but I'm not so sure that's a good idea. Instead, I want to tell a story, and if teens find truth in the story and the characters, and thus change their perspectives, well, that's a good thing. That said, I've learned from lots of e-mails from readers, mostly teen girls, that the book helped them change not their perspectives but their lives. They've told me about an abusive boyfriend they've broken up with after reading *Things Change*, especially once they see the pattern of abuse that occurs in almost all cases of domestic violence. And I guess I did want to get teens thinking about letting their hearts overrule their heads, and how sexual involvement can complicate that. I'm not writing some anti teen-sex rant, but I am showing that the real consequences of sexual involvement for most teens is not getting pregnant or contracting an STD; it's what it does to your perspective. It changes everything.

Why do you have Paul write to his father?
That served lots of purposes. First, I wanted to have two points of view and this was a technique to get Paul's story, but more important, his backstory, into the text. There's a line from Springsteen's song "Adam Raised a Cain" that burned through all of these scenes— "You're born into this life paying for the sins of somebody else's past"—and I really wanted to explore the patterns of families. I also wanted to show that, for all Paul's extroverted behavior, he's a very damaged and isolated young man. I wanted to show him reaching for a connection in his life, if only from a dead man.

Why make the parent/child relationships the way they are? Why are Jo's parents so strict? Why did you decide to make Paul's mom a born-again Christian?
Of all the stuff in the book, I think one of the biggest points of contention between myself and my editor was over how the parents, in particular, Johanna's parents, were portrayed. My defense is simply:

point of view. From the teen perspective, parents are more often villains than good guys. I wanted to show in Johanna a young woman controlled by her parents, thus it is only logical and tragic that her first significant relationship outside of her family is with another person who controls her. That is why Johanna must first "break up" with her parents before she can break up with Paul. Paul's mother had to be someone who was totally absent, and rather than have her be consumed by alcohol, I gave her religion.

Why did you have Johanna change her mind? Why didn't she leave him right away?

I actually got ripped in one review for Johanna not staying broken up with Paul after the first time he hit her. Obviously, this person had no understanding—or empathy—for women in abusive relationships. It is not easy for an adult woman to get herself out of such a situation, so how easy could it be for a teen without the same resources or experiences? I think it's implied that she tries to break up with Paul, but just can't stay away for all the obvious reasons. Also, she's got to fail at the breakup before she can go through with it for dramatic reasons, so the book doesn't end on page 90. That's the tension in the book: how will she get out of this situation?

Why did you have both Paul and Johanna tell the story rather than just one of them?

That's something going on in the book that I think a lot of people miss: you as the reader know a lot more of the bad stuff about Paul than Johanna does. Because you read his letters to his father, you get to see his anger, his drinking, and his past history, whereas Johanna doesn't know it. What I wanted by using the two points of view and letting readers learn Paul's secrets was for the reader to want to save Johanna. I want the reader to get emotionally engaged in the story and see Johanna as not so much a victim, but as a person who doesn't see there's an out-of-control car headed her way. The reader knows this and wants to pull her out of the way.

What caused Paul to become so abusive?

That's hard to say: he's grown up in an alcoholic and abusive household, so that's the world he knows. The tragedy of Paul's story is he knows this, wants to change, but cannot. He's locked into the patterns of the past. That's why I had him write the letters at a mini-storage facility filled with things from the past that neither he nor his mother can part with. Paul is abusive, he's insecure, he lacks impulse control, and he self-medicates his depression with alcohol. The primary fact of his life is that his father abandoned the family and put the weight of that on Paul's shoulders. That's why I named the mini-storage facility Atlas, after the Greek god who bore the weight of the world on his shoulders.

Why did you choose to make Bruce Springsteen Paul's favorite musician?

I'd like to say it was so I could write a check to Bruce Springsteen for the rights to use the words to "If I Should Fall Behind"—but that was only a side benefit. All the important stuff in a book has to work on more than one level. On one level, Bruce is the connection between Paul and his dad. The music has to be something his father could and would have listened to, and the things that The Boss writes about certainly would be themes that appeal to Paul's dad. More than that, the characters in Springsteen songs are true red-white-and-blue working class heroes, so they give Paul role models that are sadly lacking in his own life. Also, I wanted to show the obsession that teens have with music, but if I would have picked some contemporary band for Paul to worship, then that would really badly date the book (whereas Springsteen is forever). Finally, the themes in Springsteen's songs are the very things I want to write about. Oh, did I mention getting to write the check?

What significance does "If I Should Fall Behind" have?

While I did use lots of Springsteen lyrics, this was the only one I quoted in total. The theme of the song rips at Johanna's heart. The song is about two lovers and the realization that things go wrong in relationships ("each lover's steps fall so differently") but true love means waiting for one another. It is an idealized version of adult love and that's what Johanna aspires to. She thinks she's got to stand by Paul even through the bad times to achieve real love, but she finally learns she can't do that.

Why did you make your main character so poor?

I didn't think there were enough books about kids like Paul living on the very edge of poverty: living in trailer homes, single parent families, etc. I never want to write about teens (at least as the main characters) whose parents are doctors, lawyers, artists, etc. I want to write about working class kids in a country where the working class is disappearing. There are plenty of books, sadly and stereotypically, about black families who are poor and live in the "'hood" but not enough about kids who don't have nice clothes or new gadgets and don't drive SUVs. These kids need a voice.

When you were a teenager, what type of books did you read?

Not many, to be honest. I read magazines (*Rolling Stone*), the daily newspaper, and every magazine on professional wrestling, but not many books outside of school. I didn't read YA fiction, not because it wasn't around, but because I didn't know about it and I didn't have anyone—teachers or librarians—letting me know about it. I do recall reading *Carrie* by Stephen King (the first scene takes place in a girls' shower room; I was hooked) and then a book called *Ball Four* (Jim Bouton) which changed my life. I didn't really get hooked on reading for pleasure until after college when it was no longer something I had to do. But still today, the highlight of my week is when my *Wrestling Observer* newsletter arrives on Saturdays. That's entertainment!

What authors do you admire the most?

Rob Thomas, Chris Crutcher, and Terry Davis. I think Rob's *Rats Saw God* is the best teen novel ever, while Terry's books *If Rock and Roll Were a Machine* and *Vision Quest* are the best duo. Chris is just amazing: as a writer, as a speaker, and as a person. Finally, I do admire R. L. Stine and not just for his productivity or pocketbook. I think it is very, very hard to create a book that is entertaining to a mass audience. If you compare the number of novels written every year that everyone gushes over to those that everybody buys, I think you'll find just how difficult it is to write a bestseller, let alone one a month as he did. I think it goes without saying that I admire Bruce Springsteen greatly, and I try to put into a 200-page book the same passion that he can get into a three-minute song.

To read the interview in its entirety, visit
www.connectingya.com/thingschange
or
www.walkeryoungreaders.com

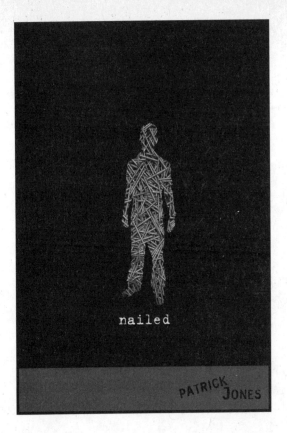

nailed

PATRICK JONES

Flint Southwestern High School is run by the jockarchy.
And Bret Hendricks could never fit into their conformity cult.
But as his safe havens disappear one by one, he may just have
to risk getting hammered in order to hold on to all that's
important to him.

Read on for a sneak peek at Patrick Jones's riveting new novel,

nailed

Two

Álex, why are we driving ourselves crazy like this?"

"Drive? I thought you weren't allowed to drive," Alex cracks back. It's his typical smartass statement. "Crazy is within walking distance for us."

Alex Shelton, my best pal, sits on a bench with me in front of the theater at Genesee Valley Mall. We pass a Camel cig between us, watching half the world go by. The better half.

"She's a seven," I say as we spy a gorgeous Gothwannabe girl, clad in black skirt and tight black T-shirt, walking by on the outskirts of her group of friends. Alex and I started this girl-rating ritual on a trip to Stratford, Ontario, for a Shakespeare festival. The number represents the number of fingers or toes we would sacrifice to any deity who could arrange for us to spend horizontal time with these unattainable angels.

"She's for you," Alex responds, yet I know none of these ladies will look at me, then simply smile. Just as well, since most of my crushes end in crushing disappointment after weeks or months of flirtation. Except for Megan the Imposter, who crushed me a whole different way last spring.

"In my dreams," I reply. We know Rule One is that no guy is ever less good-looking than the girl he's with. We keep searching for, but not finding, duos where homely horny toads like us couple with killer lookers. My fellow troglodytes must stay underground, while blond-haired blue-eyed beautiful boys like Sean, our band's drummer, roam the earth. Sean's a near ten among men, while Alex, challenged in vertical reach and clear skin, and I strive to be fives. Math may be my worst subject, but even I understand the awful arithmetic of animal attraction: guys who are fives like me don't get girls who are tens.

Rule Two is to find the outsider. Every group has an odd one out, like our gorgeous Goth girl, and that's the one we make our focus. We figure since every other wolf pack ignores the outsider, we will flatter her with attention, even if it's from a safe distance.

Rule Three is to never make eye contact. That is the difference between those of us who appreciate the captivating splendor of the female form from a respectful distance and the rude, crude bullyboys with stalker tendencies. We want love but settle for lust, or even just a look.

"Nine," Alex says, slapping my knee as a Mona Lisa Cheerleader, a girl from our school who remains unattainable to all but members of the jockarchy, walks by. The jockarchy is what we call the ball-bouncing bloc at school. Bob Hitchings, a former elementary school friend who now punches me for kicks and ridicules Alex like it was an Olympic event, is the three-letter king of that hill. At our school, these knuckle draggers score points and win rewards, but from most of us in theater, they earn only our scorn and ridicule. It's not just that they kick the ball; it's that they seem to think they deserve to walk on water and stomp on those less privileged. They're so admired at school that standing up to them isn't an option; it's a daydream.

"Very nine," I add.

"Bret, my pants are getting tighter," Alex whispers.

"No wonder they call it longing," I say. Alex cracks up. We want love and would settle for lust, but we have to make do with making each other laugh with bad puns and quick comebacks.

"Get the blood back into your brain," he says, snapping his fingers off my skull.

"Do you think they know we're doing this? Are we that obvious?" I ask.

"We should wear sunglasses," Alex says as he puts on a pair of shades to match his similar green-streaked (but naturally blond) hair, and the gold rims balance his numerous silver earrings. The sunglasses fit, since Alex is always the star of the show. He's arrogant, but he's also the smartest and funniest person I know, and a damn good friend. He's also a first-class secondhand store shopper. Today's getup is typical: the oversized black pants, a Captain Crunch T-shirt, and like me, bright green Chuck Taylor Converse All Stars; basketball shoes for two guys who can't dribble or dunk. We both prefer to hit the hardwood of the stage rather than the gym, where the pituitary cases that make up the starting five of the Flint Southwestern Spartans bang bodies. Whether it's not having a dad that beats him down, his distaste for people who don't share his taste, or his lack of fear in the face of adversity, Alex mostly avoids the problems I have swimming upstream against the high school gene pool.

"Then we'd be cool, like Sean," I say. Sean should be part of the jockarchy like his neighbor Bob Hitchings, but he's not. It's not really about sports aptitude, but a superior attitude. Sean's common love of radio-unfriendly music, smartass comments, and offbeat books and movies makes him one of us. Besides, he and Alex go way back, and loyalty matters.

"I bet those girls wouldn't even care," Alex says. "They'd prefer the validation of their beauty over the invasion of their privacy. They're all beautiful, someone should tell them. I tell you Mr. Bret Hendricks, there's not a girl in the world who isn't beautiful in some way."

"Especially Kylee Edmonds," I say. "So, Alex, tell me, what do you think Kylee is?"

He pauses to think. I've thrown him between the rock and the hard place. I'll watch him squirm while I wait for the next eye harem to pass. He takes the smoke from me and stalls.

Kylee is everything. During summer theater, Mr. Douglas invited students from Flint Central to team up for a play with us Westies. She told me she was a big deal over there, having starred in their musicals the last two years. But since we're doing *The Odd Couple,* with no singing or dancing, she opted to run the show behind the scenes as stage manager. If only she would opt for me, and let me hang on her arm like her twenty-bracelet parade.

A year older, Kylee is cynical, sarcastic, and sexy beyond belief. Petite, with a dancer's sexy body, she has a fondness for too-small tank tops and tight hip-hugging cutoffs, allowing for maximum skin exposure. This girl from Central knows how to center attention on herself, and I've gladly noticed her every second of every minute of every day. She was easy to find as the only person involved in the production with short, violet hair and a bottom lip like a plum. She never walks; she glides gracefully across the stage. Kylee's beauty is organic, original, and unbearable. After our final show in two weeks, there'll be a cast party and I'll need to make a move or lose my chance to know her. She'll be back at Central and on the outskirts of my life.

"Depends who is doing the rating," Alex finally says, but I

know he thinks that's Kylee's a total ten. Alex noticed her first but backed off, like a true trustworthy friend, once I expressed a passionate (rather than passing) interest. "I know what she is for you."

"What a succubus suck-up you are. Okay, she's a ten," I confess.

"I don't think so," Alex replies in his most annoying singsong put down voice.

"What, she's not a ten?" I ask nervously, the need for his approval noticeable.

"For you, she's a twenty!" he shouts.

"Twenty? That's all my fingers and toes! No wonder figuring out a way to approach her has me stumped!" I crack back, then we low-five. "Did you find out about a boyfriend?"

"Yes and no," Alex replies, disturbingly delighted by my discomfort.

"And?"

"Yes, she has a boyfriend," Alex says, looking away from me at the sky above, while my heart sinks six feet underground. "But I don't think she would be opposed to your advances."

"And tell me how you can predict that, Nostra-dumbass?"

"Her boyfriend's some college guy named Chad Lake."

"So what?" I ask, literally moving toward the edge of my seat.

"Well, she said, and I quote, 'He's less like a lake and more like a puddle.'"

"What does that mean?" I ask, knowing it will be Kylee-style: smart and sarcastic.

"She said he's more like a puddle because he's shallow and casts a nice reflection," Alex says, cracking us both up and drawing unwanted attention to our observation outpost, just as a major ten passes. I hear my heart beat faster, pumping blood south, as

I point the girl out to him. This girl is like a flag: red hair, white T-shirt, and blue jeans. She makes us stand at attention.

"I didn't realize you liked redheads," Alex comments.

"Don't you know by now what kind of girls I like?"

"None, if you ask your dad!" Alex chortles. My dad thinks both Alex and I are gay.

"I don't ask my dad anything," I say sharply. Alex's dad died when he was ten, and I never tell him how much I envy him for that; almost as much as I envy his ability to write songs.

"Well, you don't seem to have one type," Alex says, stating the obvious.

"I like redheads, blonds, brunettes, and Goths with black hair. Of late, I find that I'm especially interested in dancers with violet hair, and I'm sure if I saw a bald girl go by I would find something to like about her."

"I'll be on the lookout for one of those," Alex says with a sly grin.

"You think girls do this?" I ask, trying to distract myself.

"I hope not. We're not tens by any means," he says, stating the vicious and the obvious.

"Well, except for Sean," I acknowledge.

"Maybe our band should be called the Blond Shy Guy and the Multicolored Mangy Miscreants rather than Radio-Free Flint," Alex says.

"Maybe," I mutter, totally befuddled by the unfairness of beauty.

"Or how about the Mental Babes?" Alex cracks, but I don't respond. Last spring, there was a story about the theater club in the school paper. There was a quote from this popular-crowd girl, Becca Levy, calling me a "mental babe." I'm a successful student, an improving actor, a kick-ass bass player and energetic lead singer in my band. I try to be a good brother to my younger sister, Robin, even though she's twelve now and wants nothing to do with her weird older brother. Despite my problems with Dad at home and Bob Hitchings at school, the last few years have been a sweet life. But this "mental babe" memory sours me. It hurts even more coming from Becca, who, like me, is smarter than she is pretty. I've secretly always had a hard spot for her. Mental babe? Kill me now.

"I bet Kylee thinks that about me too," I say sadly, just as Sean joins us. Looking at Sean, I wonder if I was more like him and less like Alex, if I'd have more of a chance with Kylee.

"What, you don't think any girl would lose a finger over you?" Alex asks.

"Most just give me the finger," I say with a laugh.

Sean jabs me in the ribs, then points at a blond walking by. "She's tenriffic!"

PATRICK JONES

has been connecting teens with books since he graduated from college. He is a nationally respected young-adult librarian, the author of several critically acclaimed books for YA experts, and a popular speaker for teens and librarians. *Things Change* was Patrick's first novel for teens. He was born and raised in Flint, Michigan, and currently lives in the Minneapolis area.

Visit his Web site at
www.connectingya.com/thingschange